John W. Berry

Uniac: His Life, Struggle, and Fall

John W. Berry

Uniac: His Life, Struggle, and Fall

ISBN/EAN: 9783743371002

Manufactured in Europe, USA, Canada, Australia, Japa

Cover: Foto ©Raphael Reischuk / pixelio.de

Manufactured and distributed by brebook publishing software (www.brebook.com)

John W. Berry

Uniac: His Life, Struggle, and Fall

Yours very truly
E. H. Uniac.

UNIAC:

HIS

LIFE, STRUGGLE, AND FALL.

BY

JOHN W. BERRY.

BOSTON:
ALFRED MUDGE & SON, PRINTERS.
1871.

U N I A C :

his

LIFE, STRUGGLE, AND FALL.

BY

JOHN W. BERRY.

BOSTON:
ALFRED MUDGE & SON, PRINTERS.
1871.

Stereotyped by ALFRED MUDGE & SON,
84 School Street, Boston.

Dedication.

TO MY SAINTED FATHER

NOW IN HEAVEN,

THE MEMORY OF WHOSE LIFE OF PURITY

HAS BEEN TO ME

AN INSPIRATION

IN THE

DIRECTION OF EVERY GOOD ACTION,

I REVERENTLY

DEDICATE THIS BOOK.

INTRODUCTION.

I WAS a personal friend of the subject of this book, and knew him in private as well as in public life. I saw day by day his character and talents displayed to their best advantage. After he had charmed thousands by his power and eloquence, and had been instrumental in saving many from the drunkard's awful fate, his fall on the 17th of March, 1869, in the State of Connecticut, was as unexpected as it was sad.

From that dark day, I, with other friends, followed him, trying to help him in his struggles against the terrible power of appetite; and after we had the joy of seeing him stand up once more in all the strength of his true manhood, I became his constant companion until his sad death.

A few weeks after this event, I became convinced that the story of his life ought to go before the world, believing that if read by the young men of the country it . would do good. I conferred with other personal friends and with prominent temperance men, and all agreed as to the importance of having it accomplished. With many misgivings in regard to my ability to do justice to the subject, and with a prayer to God for assistance, I began the work.

I have endeavored to trace his eventful life with fidelity to truth; and, as as far as possible, have gathered from his own words the thread of his life's struggle, and have presented thrilling and eloquent extracts from his writings and best speeches, which show the man better than any words of mine. In explanation of the long delay in the appearance of this work, we wish to state that it was owing to the necessary and unavoidable waiting for some matters absolutely essential to the completion of the same. And we beg, also, to apologize for the many errors of matter and manner herein contained.

If, in the reading of these pages, any poor, tempted heart shall be made stronger to battle against intemperance, or one young man saved from the curse of the cup, I shall be more than repaid for any effort of mine. I cannot close without thanking the friends who have kindly assisted me in the way of furnishing facts and dates.

JOHN W. BERRY.

CONTENTS.

UNIAC:

HIS

LIFE, STRUGGLE, AND FALL.

CHAPTER I.

BIRTH — CHILDHOOD — LEAVING HOME — ARRIVAL IN NEW
YORK — ASSOCIATIONS, ETC.

WHILE it may not be of much interest to know the details of the early life of UNIAC, we have thought a few prominent facts connected with his childhood of importance, as illustrating and explaining his after career. Sometimes, in the early years of a man's life, we can detect incidents that shape and mould all his future.

Edward H. Uniac was born in the town of Waterford, Ireland, on the eighth day of July, 1833. His parents were Irish, of the Protestant faith, and members of the Church of England. His father was a colonel in the British army, and is represented as being an Irish gentleman of the old school, very strict in his family government, and sometimes almost severe. In Mr. Uniac's diary, he speaks of his parents, home, and youth, as follows: "I had a mother to direct me in the way of piety, and a good Christian father to advise and guide me, and every Sabbath found me at the foot of the altar, filling up my little soul with divine truth and love. My light

shone brightly then, my days rolled by like a smooth-
faced river, my happiness was complete."

This extract is enough to satisfy us that his home
training was good, and that his young feet were led in
very different paths from those dark and dangerous ones
through which he afterwards walked.

There have been two stories told in regard to his leaving
home, which we will give, without vouching for the truth
of either of them. At the time of the O'Connell trouble
in Ireland, in the year 1848, Edward was attending a
school to which was attached a military department, and
although a mere boy he drilled in secret, after dark, a
number of men who sympathized with O'Connell.

An order was issued about this time by the British
Government, to arrest all who had assisted in giving military instructions to the rebels. As soon as the facts
connected with the drilling of the men came to the ears
of Uniac's father, he hastened to the school, took his son
away, and, as the best means of saving him from arrest
and punishment under the law, secured him a passage on
a vessel bound for New York.

The other story says, that his father was in the habit
of whipping his children, and after one of these severe
punishments, Edward resolved to leave home without his
father's knowledge, and did so, after having secured passage for America.

It is not of importance for us to know which of these
stories is true, for the information in our possession is
too meagre to dwell long on this part of his life. We
know that he arrived in the city of New York, with his
future to make by his own hands.

A little incident occurred on his passage, and as it has a bearing on his future, we will give it.   It was customary in those days to supply sailors with "grog," and once when they were drinking it, one of the men offered the boy a taste from his dipper.   In speaking of the incident, Uniac said: "I did not dare to refuse, and took a few swallows," and as he passed the dipper back, the old sailor said, "That boy knows what is good." And Uniac said, "I confess I did like the taste of it, and though the sailors did not offer me any more during the voyage, I used to often wish they would."

Some people believe that certain persons are born with an appetite for strong drink, something which they inherit and take to naturally, and there seems to be good grounds for believing this to be true.   Had the drinking of the few swallows of grog — referred to above — been distasteful to the boy, the remembrance of it would have been unpleasant, and he would have had no inclination or desire to repeat it.

Some men have become drunkards, who were first fascinated with the effect, rather than the taste; but when both the taste, and the desire for the effect, are strong, the individual who possesses them is, indeed, unfortunate.   From the incident referred to, and the testimony of Uniac in after years, we may infer that he was thus unfortunate in having this natural desire for that which was the bane of his life.

One evening Uniac spoke of his childhood days, and said: "Whatever has come to me through the evil of intemperance is not owing to any wrong influence connected with my home, for though in those days it was the fashion to use wine at the table, I do not remember ever seeing any at my father's."

In a letter written when he was struggling with his enemy, after speaking feelingly of some dear friends of his youth, he says, " When I think of the advantages that were presented to me in my young days, and feel how much I might have accomplished, had I been true to my home education, I feel keenly the truth of Whittier's words, when he says, —

> ' Of all sad words of tongue or pen,
> The saddest are these, it might have been.' "

When we think how small an event changes the course of a man's life, how tenderly careful should we be in regard to the position in which we place the young ! Consider the difference in this man's life, caused by his leaving the home associations !

There is something mysterious about Uniac's first days in this country. We have not been able to get much in the way of dates, to assist us in following his life very closely at this time, and are therefore obliged to present what we have, in a somewhat disconnected manner. In one of his lectures, he alluded to his native land as follows : " Some people seem to regard it as a crime to be an Irishman ; if so, I am a criminal. My grandfather, and also my great-grandfather, were born in the south of France, while my father, and all my ancestors on the maternal side, were born in Ireland ; so that I am a branch shooting out from a truly noble Celtic trunk, that shot up centuries ago in the groves of this green isle of the sea. My love for my native country is as pure as a child's love for his mother ; and, though I left her quite young, I have not forgotten her green fields and noble-hearted people.

" America is the wife and choice of my adoption. Every law, human and divine, bids me protect both.

" I would fight for Ireland if I had the opportunity ; I have fought beneath the folds of your banner, as it fluttered in the breeze, and entwined its stripes around the Irish harp, and scattered the radiance of its stars over the green field of the Irish standard. Side by side they fought, on they pressed, o'er the dead and dying, through the scattered sides of the foe, never shrinking from the post assigned them, — standing firm, Irish and American, until victory was won, or the contest decided."

The above beautiful extract shows that he never forgot the home of his childhood.

He was probably supplied with one or two letters of introduction to some prominent gentlemen in this country ; and after a pleasant passage across the Atlantic, landed in the great city of New York, with hardly a friend in the country. Innocent and pure, fresh from the blessings and benedictions of a Christian home, he stood in the midst of crime and temptation of every kind. What a position for any youth to occupy, who wanted to be true to virtue and temperance !

With thousands on his right and on his left ready to tempt and lead to ruin and destruction, with untold numbers of dram-shops on every street, how is it possible that he, or any young man similarly situated, shall be able to pass through this furnace of vice, and come out without the smell of smoke **upon** his garments !

How long he remained alone, or what was his daily
occupation, we do not know. Neither have we any
letters telling much about this period in the life of our
subject.

Any one who has visited the institutions on Blackwell's
Island, and noticed the hundreds of bright and intelli-
gent-looking boys confined there for various crimes, must
have felt impressed with the dangers that beset the youth
of our great cities. In conversing with some of the
officers of the institution, we found that many who were
inmates, although mere boys, had contracted the habit
of using intoxicating drinks as a beverage. The street
education of our larger towns and cities is becoming
worse and worse. The indecent literature in the form
of illustrated sheets, together with the notoriety given
by respectable journals to races of every description, the
street gambling carried on under the name of gift enter-
prises, and the desire of managers of what is called
variety theatres, to cater to the lower tastes and pas-
sions of the people, all tend to demoralize the young and
rising generation.

What shall be done to purify and make safe our
streets, is a question fraught with deep interest to the
future of this nation. Let any one take a stroll after
the lamps are lighted, and survey our cities by gas-light,
and they will be convinced that it is not safe, in the present condition of affairs, to have a police department
appointed by, and responsible to, the voters of these
cities for their position and support. It is true that the
attempt to govern and control these municipalities is
really a failure, while the officers are dependent on the

votes and influence of keepers of brothels and dram-
shops. When the public sentiment is educated up to the
point that shall demand the enactment of sound and
wholesome laws for the prevention and punishment of
crime, and sustain the authorities in the enforcement of
the same, then shall we see our large cities well and
properly governed.

Uniac probably did not remain in New York City but
a few weeks, for not very long after his arrival we hear
of him at Troy in the same State. One of the letters of
introduction that he had, was to a gentleman residing in
that city.

His boyhood days were doubtless like those of other
boys, except, as he often said, he used to wish he was
old enough to join the social gatherings where the wine-
cup went round; thus showing that his natural inclination was tending in the direction of wine drinking.

We are not able to tell who were his companions at
this time; for, while Uniac was confiding in his nature,
he seldom mentioned the time of which we are writing.
Could we know the every-day history of those youthful
days, the temptations of every hour that came to him,
we might be able to tell when he first formed the habit
of drinking, and found himself engaged in the contest
that was to be his life's struggle. Who can tell the heartaches, the cares, self-denial, and glorious fighting necessary to a man of his nature?

A man of this character is dependent on the circumstances that surround him for his success in life. Had Uniac
passed his youthful days in the society of temperate and
virtuous people, his struggle would have been less severe,

and his victory almost certain. We cannot estimate too highly how much our boys are affected by their associations in the tender years of life, when they are being moulded for all their future.

Every mother who has sent her son into the world to seek his fortune, feels the great importance of good surroundings for her boy, in the direction of having for his companions those who are pledged to temperance and virtue.

In all our great cities we need attractions for young men and youth, in the way of innocent amusements. If a dance-house, with bar-room attached, is opened on one corner of a street, let efforts be made to open a pleasant and attractive place of amusement on the other side of the same street, under the control of Christian men and women. Have a reading-room, but do not stop there ; have also a billiard-room and a bowling-alley, where they can have an opportunity to play these games, — harmless in themselves, — and not be tempted to drink. We ought not to let the enemies of temperance have the only places where men can indulge in these kinds of sports, and thus draw in many young men who would not go there if they could find anywhere else a place to indulge their taste for these amusements.

Young men — many of them — are of a social nature, and like the society of women ; and if our Christian women do not give an opportunity to these homeless youth to enjoy the society of the pure women, the temptation to seek the impure will be great. Uniac, in one of his lectures, in referring to a period of his life when he was alone in Troy, said, " O, how often did I wish I could come under the influence of good women, to feel their purifying presence ; and many a night as I wandered through the street, and saw the light of happy firesides gleaming out warm and bright, I have been almost tempted to open the door of some home and walk in." He also related the following story. "One Christmas eve, when the snow was coming down rapidly, I had only a low, dingy room in a dirty house ; and as I heard the vesper bells ringing out on the night air, I could not stay where I was, and so, putting on my old worn overcoat, I started out on to the street. I met people hurrying hither and thither, all bent on happiness ; now would come a group of merry, laughing children, hastening to take part in the pleasures of a Christmas tree ; and now comes a party of young men, talking and laughing ; while I wandered up and down the street, looking into this window, and standing in that doorway, wishing and hoping that before another Christmas rolled round, I too might also be free from the temptation of street life. O, how I felt that night ! and O, how many young men feel to-night as I felt then ! Can we not help them ? "

Uniac's experience at this time has its repetition in the history of hundreds and thousands of the noblest and best of our young men.

Bellows has painted a beautiful picture, called the "Echo"; in the foreground is a boat containing two soldiers and their friends, who have been out to meet and welcome them to "Home, sweet home." One of them, an officer, pillows his weary head on his mother's lap ; the other, a cavalry trumpeter, with his affianced by his

2

side, has just played "Home, sweet home," and all
seem to be listening to catch the echo of that dear old
strain, as it comes reverberating over hill and through
dell, making all nature vocal with sweetest music. In
the distance may be seen bonfires, mingling their
brightness with the golden rays of setting day, all seeming to be a glorious ending to the sad day of gloom that
had long hung over our country. As we looked at that
picture, we thought there are others, who have been
fighting the battle of life for more than four years, who
have been wounded often ; and they wander up and down
our streets, and listen for the echo of home language and
home virtues. Let them but hear it, never so faintly,
and many of them will turn from the error of their ways,
and be men once more.

Shall we speak the word? Will we make an effort to
save the homeless and friendless? If we will do this
duty, God will reward, and Heaven will bless our
efforts.

CHAPTER II.

SCHOOL DAYS — ADMITTED TO THE BAR — COMPANIONS — FORMATION OF DRINKING HABITS, ETC.

IT was in the city of Troy, or somewhere in that immediate vicinity, that he attended school for two or three years. While going to school, he frequently went to the court-house, and was much interested in the trial cases. He had such an excellent memory, that after listening to the argument of some attorney, he would go home and repeat all the leading points; in fact, he showed such a love for the law, that he was advised to select that profession, and did so, and soon after entered the office of an attorney, and began to prepare himself for the practice of the law.

From the most reliable information, we feel convinced that during these years, while a student at law, he formed the habit of drinking regularly. This must be so, from the fact that about the time he was admitted to the bar, he received the sad intelligence of his mother's death, and years afterwards, when speaking of this event, he remarked that his conscience smote him, for he knew that he had been doing that which she would not have approved. But, in a letter written years after, he dates his downward career a few years later; but doubtless the seeds were sown while he mingled with the young and fashionable portion of society. We should remember that at that time the temperance reform had not made great progress in the direction of influencing public opinion, or diminishing the traffic in intoxicating liquors, and therefore the society that a young student or lawyer mingled in, was probably of that kind that admitted and countenanced social drinking. We have proof of this in the following extract from one of his letters : "I well remember the effect that some of the evening parties used to have on me and other students, in the direction of headaches consequent on champagne drinking." Although much of what is called the best society of to-day place wine on the table, it is going more and more out of fashion, and is being banished from homes every year. This was never more noticeable than during the present season at Washington ; and had a popular writer, who began an article for the "Atlantic Monthly" with the statement, that "Teetotallers confess their failure," read correctly the signs of the times, and noted the substantial progress of teetotalism, he would have found it impossible for an intelligent teetotaller anywhere, to have admitted anything like a failure, where there has been so much success.

Uniac said, that during his temperance work in Massachusetts, he took occasion, while visiting New York, to look around among those who were his former associates, and he was surprised at the change that had taken place. Shops were closed in many instances, and a generation of drunkards seemed to have passed away, while young and active business men had taken their places, and he could see a decided gain for temperance and morality. He seemed to be very much impressed with one fact, and that was the large number who had died since he knew the locality. This is noticeable everywhere among drinking men. A lawyer who has practised in one of our large cities for twenty odd years, said that right in the square where his office was, he could count twenty lawyers, who started in life when he did, with hopes as bright and prospects as fair, who had long since found an early grave, through the effects of intemperance. We do not fully realize these appalling facts, so quiet and insidious are the workings of this evil in our very midst.

Uniac told one thrilling story of a companion of these dark days. While he was reading law, he became acquainted with a young man, a graduate of a college, with fine natural abilities, who was his constant friend, and who, like him, had a powerful appetite with which he was struggling. When he graduated from college, his abilities were of so marked a character, that all who knew him confidently predicted, that before many years he would occupy a high position in the profession : and, for the first two or three years that he practised law, he was very successful. But his appetite grew stronger and stronger, and his efforts to resist it were less effectual. He had married a·lady of a good family, and by the union a little boy was born. Not to dwell on the details, suffice it to say, that from continual drinking and exposure, it became evident he had contracted that slow but fatal disease, consumption. When he came near his death, he called his friends around him, and said he had but one request to make, and that was, as he had disappointed the hopes and expectations of all, and had disgraced his wife and child while living, " When I die,

in some obscure spot in the old graveyard of my native
town, let me rest; but raise not a stone, or carve a line,
to mark the place where I lie; for if I disgraced you
while living, I would in death be forgotten." And should
the reader wander through the sacred spot, doubtless he
would find nothing to note the resting-place of this ruined
man, not even the raised mound, for time has long since
levelled that. But once every year, when the flowers
bloom, with uncovered head, above that spot a youth
stands, and gathers, from the remembrance of his father's
struggle, inspiration and strength to stand firm by the
vow and promise to touch not, taste not, anything that
shall intoxicate, made as he listened to this sad story at
his mother's knee.

There is a story almost the counterpart to the above,
told feelingly to the people by an earnest and eloquent
temperance speaker in Massachusetts, who concludes it
by saying, that in Plymouth County there is a lonely
grave, unnamed and unknown, where lies buried one of
the most brilliant and gifted scholars, cut off in the prime
of his manhood by this same great destroyer.

Uniac would often sit for hours, and tell incidents of
the ruin of those he loved, while the tears would run
down his cheeks, and with trembling voice he would say,
"I pray God to give me victory in this struggle for life,
character, and all that is dear."

We do not expect to show that at this time of his life
he had no faults, perhaps other than those that come from
intemperance; but whatever they were, however aggravated their character, we feel sure that those living, who
remember these days and who may have been associated

with him by the tenderest ties, will agree with us when
we say, that had it not been for the intoxicating cup, his
condition would have been brighter, happier, and better.

We do not know as his present every-day life differed
from hundreds and thousands of those who are similarly
situated. But his brilliant talents were so prominently
before the public, and his struggle so manifest, that no
young man can read the sad tale, and not feel that it is
dangerous for him to tamper with that which ruined
Uniac.

In a letter written to a friend, he says, "You will
remember, my dear friend, that in our talk last night I
spoke of the days when I had a happy home; and you
must have observed how reticent I was in regard to
incidents and scenes of which my heart seemed to be full.
I thought perhaps you might misunderstand my manner,
and I just drop you a line to say that I have no friend to
whom I would sooner confide anything connected with
my life's story. But there are some things too sacred to
lift the veil, and disclose to other eyes than those immediately interested. When a man looks on any work that
has cost him years of toil, and at last has the satisfaction of seeing it in its perfection, and learns to love it as
he gazes on its beauty, and then in a little while beholds
it shattered and ruined at his feet, and feels that he has
accomplished this ruin all himself, he must feel something as I do when I see the fondest hopes of my life —
home, domestic happiness, and all — a wreck at my feet;
and I cannot talk freely of those days when the storm
of intemperance had not shattered the idols of my heart.
And this is my excuse for seeming indifferent in regard

to the line of conversation your remark suggested. I
feel I must 'let the dead past bury its dead,' and that for
me, with God's help, the future must atone in some measure for the disappointments, broken vows, and shattered
hopes of the past. I sometimes feel the truth of the
poet's words, when he says, —

> 'What peaceful hours I once enjoyed,
>   How sweet their memory still;
> But they have left an aching void
>   The world can never fill.'"

When he referred to these days, tears would fill his
eyes, and he would often say,—

"O God! had I stopped before I became a slave to
this power!"

In a letter written to an intimate friend, he says : —

"I have often thought of my life at the time after I
was admitted to the bar, and wondered that I had any
business at all; for I had began to drink so much that I
could not attend to my business well."

This shows that at this hour the enemy of his life
had begun to get the better of his manhood and
virtue.

We found the following note among some old
papers : —

"DEAR NED,— You got through with your business at the court-
house to-day very nicely, but I am frank to say, if you had taken one
glass less, or drank none at all, you would have done quite as well.
What do you think? Yours,   JIM."

This note was undoubtedly from some young companion, and he had kept it with his papers; and as it

was worn with much handling, perhaps he had looked at it, and thought how much he would have been saved from, had he heeded the warning this implied; while on the back of it was written these words, in Uniac's hand, "Poor Jim! had he but followed the advice his good heart prompted him to give me, he would not now be filling the grave of a drunkard."

This tells us why he valued this piece of paper. Who shall ever know the struggles of this man who feared for his friend? How often do we find people giving advice to their friends, when they are in more danger themselves!

Some men who have the appetite for liquor have lost the power to do what they feel to be right; they cannot say "No," when invited to drink; and more young men can trace their ruin to this custom of "treating," than to almost any other influence. Uniac has often said, when referring to those days when he was at the bar as a young lawyer, that he would get up in the morning, and make a solemn promise to abstain, and would be able to keep his resolve, until pressed to drink by some friend, who seemed to regard his refusal as an insult to his invitation, and he would yield.

A story is related of a gentleman who was in the company of Jews for a few months, and everywhere they went, they invited the gentleman to drink wine and other drinks of this nature. He told them he did not need the drink, he did not like it, but all to no purpose; they insisted, and he yielded. The time soon came when they returned the visit; and before they arrived, he had cooked a large quantity of bacon; and when they

came, he politely invited them to partake of the same.
Of course they refused, insisting that they did not believe in eating it; but the gentleman reminded them that
when he was their guest, they insisted on his drinking,
when he was not thirsty, that which he did not like,
and that they felt insulted by his refusal; and now he
demanded of them that they should eat whenever he felt
like offering it to them.

And it is just as reasonable and proper to require a
man to eat every time you ask him, just what you feel
like presenting, as to expect a man to drink when he
does not need it, or believe in taking it.

The following, from Uniac, will show how matters
stood with him, when he began the practice of law : —

"Well, I have chosen my profession, and have in
reality begun the work of life. Now, on what are my
hopes founded, that I shall meet with success worthy
of my manhood? This is my birthday, a kind of mile-
stone in the journey of life, a place to stop and consider
the past, and gather strength and courage for the future.
I am young in years, yet I seem old in sins. How
gladly, gladly would I blot out many scenes in my life's
history ! To-day, my mind runs back to those blessed
birthdays I spent at home, under the influence of a dear
mother, whose life was one of devotion to her children.
How differently am I situated now ! How much of the
world have I seen in a few years ! I feel almost disheartened, and ready to give up the struggle before I
have begun it. I make the highest and the firmest resolves, and go forth to keep and sustain them; I meet
with temptations, and am lost. My nature is peculiarly

sensitive; I do not like to give or take offence, and am easily persuaded to yield to the tempter. Now on this day, the starting of a new year of my life, I pray God to give me strength to do my whole duty, to keep me from yielding to temptation, to make me a man, standing in his holy image."

The above was written on the leaf of an old book, and was kept in his desk for many years.

He was at times very despondent, and felt his condition deeply. We cannot reflect on what he afterwards passed through, without feeling that he must have had many sad and gloomy hours. It is a remarkable fact, that all through his life, amid the darkest days, he seemed to have hours when he would fully realize his true position, thus proving that he never gave himself up to his condition, but kept up the fight heroically, battling with a terrible power.

It is true, in the case of every drinking man; that he has seen, or will see, the time when he has the power to stop the tasting of the intoxicating cup, but not the will; and soon the hour comes when the will is good, but the power is gone. O, what an awful position is a man in then! As we have seen Uniac on his knees, crying, "O, my God! must I die a drunkard?" as great drops of sweat stood out on his forehead, we have felt that this man had indeed the will to reform, but, alas! he had lost the power. When he was writing on his birthday, doubtless he had more power than will. He had not will enough to meet his companions, and refuse; but he saw the time afterwards, when he would have been willing to have lost all his friends if he could have had

the strength to resist the craving of his own appetite.
Many to-day are debating the expediency, rather than
the question, of right. "Will it be best for my friends,
for my business?" is the question men are asking themselves, and are not looking to the time which is coming
with many of them, when friends and everything else
will forsake them, and they will be left powerless to
act.

Soon after the birthday referred to, Uniac pledged
himself not to drink any more, and for a time everything
went well. Business began to increase, and we find the
following in his diary: "I am doing well; I have kept
myself free from the cup for sometime, and this morning
I saw the sun rise, and it seemed to me the world never
looked so beautiful as now, and the birds never sang
half so sweetly. O, though I have not sunk so low as
many, I feel I have lost much of the beauty of earth by
clouding my vision with a false curtain of supposed
pleasures." If now some good angel had unfolded to his
view, and shown him the future, painted out the blots
and tears, the sad pictures that were to make up his life
unless he continued on in this new way, how would he
have changed the painting of his after career! how much
brighter and fresher would he have presented it to the
world! and in after years, instead of saying mournfully,
"It might have been," would have stood up in his manhood, and said, "It has been."

CHAPTER III.

MARRIAGE — BRIGHT AND DARK DAYS — FAMILY RELATIONS.

HE had now become acquainted with an estimable lady, to whom, after a courtship of some little time, he was married.

We would gladly pass over this portion of his life, and remain silent on everything connected with his wife, marriage, and children, did we not desire to tell the whole story, for the purpose of showing the utter hideousness of the demon intemperance, — to show to what depths of degradation it will carry a man, even to the condition of disgracing home, and all that is holy and sacred about the family circle ; for it seems not only to steal away the brains, but the heart, and all those high and noble feelings that lift a man above the meaner things of earth. It would seem natural, even though a man had contracted bad habits while he was young and alone in the world, that when he promised to love, honor, and protect a noble-hearted woman who was as pure as snow, he would reform altogether. But when we blame a man for doing what looks to us a terribly wrong and wicked act, we should not fail to remember, that only those who have had the bitter experience, with a fearfully depraved appetite, can begin to comprehend what a man will do or

leave undone, in order to satisfy the cravings of what
has become a diseased body. The testimony of nearly
all who have come under this curse, proves that there
are times when at the risk of all they hold dear on earth,
or hope for hereafter, they will have drink. We have
heard a celebrated orator, who has passed through this
fiery ordeal, say that he has seen whole days when he
would have been willing to have placed his right hand
into a scorching flame, and taken it out burnt to a crisp,
if thereby he could have satisfied his fearful appetite.
So in considering the subject of this book, his relation
with his wife and dearest friends, finding him of good
natural qualities when not under the power of his appetite, fulfilling all the duties of husband and father, and
utterly disregarding them at other times, let us remember
the power that controlled him, think of his desperate
struggles to free himself, and from this standpoint judge
him. After his marriage he continued the practice of law,
and from his statement of the business he transacted, he
must have met with decided success, and had as bright
prospects as any young man then at the bar. Unfortunately for him, many of his best clients (in a financial
view) were engaged in the liquor business; and as a
natural consequence, his whole association soon became
with men of this character. He felt that he was being
bound hand and foot, and often resolved to free himself
from its thraldom. He regarded this period of his life
as among the darkest of all his days, for now the star of
hope gleamed but faintly. He had those he loved, and
who cared for him, but of course he soon began to neglect his business, and it gradually left him; for even

those who are engaged in the rum business, are not
willing to trust men with *their* business, who were under
the influence of their goods.

By his marriage two children were born, one of which
is still living in the city of Philadelphia; and although
her father was often overcome by his life's enemy, she
need not blush when she reads the record of work he
accomplished for God and humanity, while he labored
for temperance. We will not weary the reader by going
into the details of his condition, and the incidents of his
every-day life at this time. While he was in the midst
of his drinking habits, and had probably become somewhat reduced in finances, he received news of the death
of his father, by which he came into possession of about
thirty-two thousand dollars. This money, coming at
this critical time in his life, was like fuel to a burning
building. If we have made a mistake in regard to the
time when this happened, it will not matter, as there is
no doubt but what he did receive this amount at *some*
period when he was nearly under the control of his appetite. He had also spent about eight thousand dollars
which he had saved, so that about forty thousand dollars
(a large fortune in those days) was squandered—yes,
worse than squandered—all because the demon within
him was crying, Give! Give! Give!

These dark days were not without their bright spots;
but from what we saw of him after his last fall, and
remember the influences that were trying to save him,
and think to what depths he went, over the prayers and
entreaties of his friends, we can estimate something of
his situation before he became associated with temper-

ance people, and was left almost to his own destruction.
We do not mean to give the impression, that those of his
friends who knew him well and were associated with him
did not do all they could to assist him. It is but just
that we should say, that we scarcely know anything in
regard to the time he was living with his wife, nor have
we sought to, feeling that it would not be of interest.
And did we attempt to say anything, we might say
something that would do injustice to him, and to those
who are living, who were intimately connected with this
time. It was necessary that mention should be made of
it, as, at the time of his death, the press throughout the
land made some statements in regard to the matter,
which were calculated to give a wrong impression.

Doubtless this period in his life's history was filled
with doubt and misgivings as to all his future, for now
his wife began to despair of saving him, and to consider the question of her duty in the matter of a separation. We have been told by a gentleman who knew
Uniac when he had a family and home, that he often
heard his friends remark, that his would indeed be a
happy family and pleasant home, were it not for his
intemperate drinking. How often at this day do we
hear the same remark in regard to homes all around us !
It is the skeleton in hundreds of families ; it is the foundation of two thirds of the trouble between men and
women, that result in the breaking-up of domestic happiness, and home itself.

The following touching story, told by a wife of a
drunkard, ought to sink deep into the hearts of all who
read it.

"I was born in the State of Vermont, in a little village away up in the mountains. My husband was born near my home; we grew up together. I loved him, and he seemed to love me. When we became of age, he proposed to me, and we were married. I never knew he used liquor. I had seen on one or two occasions that he appeared to like cider, but so many very good people said there was no harm in drinking that mild drink, of course I thought nothing of it. Two years after our marriage, we went to New York to live. My husband entered a store, and we began life in the hope of meeting with success; but his love for cider grew into a desire for something stronger; and it is the old story; he went from bad to worse, until position, friends, and everything was gone. O friends, if you could only see what I have seen, or feel what I have felt, as I labored to save him I loved, I know you would pity me. He changed, O how much I can hardly tell! Once handsome, neat, and clean, he became bloated, dirty, and untidy; and when the cold winds of winter beat the snow in my face, I have wandered up and down the streets of New York, trying to find him. But at last relief came. And alone with him, as he lay on a heap of straw, in a low dingy room, I held his head, as his poor, ruined, wasted life ebbed away. And just before he died, consciousness came back, and he opened his eyes, and looking up in my face, said, —

"'Well, Mary, it's 'most over with me; I shall not worry and fret you much longer. I am going, I hope, where the weak are not tempted, where I shall find rest and friends.'"

3

Here she stopped, for tears choked her utterance. After waiting a moment, she proceeded : —

"I felt that he grew weaker, his voice also trembled, and he spoke with much difficulty ; but, thank God, he did say, 'Mary, I have sometimes, in my hours of madness, thought of our dear, happy home by the Green Mountains, and O, had not this tempter entered it, we might have always been as happy as we were then.' He faltered, asked me to kiss him, and his spirit had floated out on to the great sea of eternity ; and I, a weak girl, stood alone in that great city, with —" And here she drew herself up to her full height, while her eyes flashed fire, as she exclaimed, "Yes, with my murdered husband, murdered by the rum power of this country. And ever since that time, when I have stood above his grave in our old church-yard, I have vowed to do all in my power to crush this evil, and, God helping me, I will do it."

How many wives suffer in silence, God only knows ; and when we call the roll of heroes and heroines of earth, let us not forget those noble women who are slowly wearing their lives away, in devotion to those to whom they have pledged their love. If we do this, we shall see that it is not on the battle-field, or the world's highest pinnacles, that we behold the grandest types of God's image ; but down deep amid the lowlands of life, among its mists and shadows, through the darkness which surrounds them, we gaze on the patient, suffering human beings, who are dying that those they love may live ; and when they shall be seen by the light of heaven, their grandeur and beauty of soul will fill us with wonder and delight.

CHAPTER IV.

STRUGGLE RAGING — DESPERATE EFFORTS TO REFORM —
LETTER TO COMPANION — INCIDENTS.

THE struggle with his appetite had now really com-
menced, and it is due to his manhood and memory that
we should here record his desperate attempts to rid himself from the power of the demon who seemed to have
control of his every action, even at this early period.

We do not desire to leave the impression that there
were not at *this* time bright spots in his sky of life, for
there were months when he would not touch a drop, nor
that he was different than other young men who drank
with him. But the insidious approaches and deceptive
manner by which this enemy sometimes makes his attacks,
would overthrow him. We will give from his own lips,
as nearly as possible, one of his struggles, and what led
to his overthrow.

One night after going home from one of his drinking
spells, he awoke with a burning thirst, and got up to
procure some water, — then went to the window.

It was a bright moonlight night, and he saw a woman
with a young man on her arm, endeavoring to persuade
him to go home. When near his window, the young
man stoutly refused to go any farther.

Uniac opened the window, and heard the woman say,

"Edward, you are my only son; *do* go home with me, or you will break my heart." It so affected the man at the window, that he closed it, and thought of his own dear mother, and of what would be her feelings could she see him going on in his mad career; and, dropping on his knees, with the pale moon looking down, he prayed God for strength to begin once more the struggle to free himself from the slavery of rum. He had a terrible fight for weeks, hope came back, and the future looked brighter and better than it had for a long time, when one evening he was invited to attend a social party, and accepted the invitation. While there, when he was feeling warm from the crowd which was present, a gentleman offered him a glass of wine which was being passed round.

He struggled with his appetite for a moment, and refused; when a lady friend, noticing his abstinence, took a glass, stepped forward to him, and said, "Mr. Uniac, I know you will drink my health." It would have been hard for any young man in that position to have said "No"; but for him, with his natural gallantry and his gnawing appetite craving it, the struggle was over. Wine the victor! the resolve, the man, conquered! The rest is soon told. After one glass he drank another. Who can estimate the evil accomplished by this simple act? There ought to go up in our land, a voice to be heard in every home, crying out for the banishment of this destroyer from the social circle. In the name of the hundreds and thousands of young men who date their ruin from it, and because of the power it has to make drinking seem respectable, we demand it!

Young men who have faced the cannon on the field of

battle, have not had courage to say "No" under like circumstances. Uniac used to tell a story of a man who is
now in one of our state-prisons, that so well and thrillingly shows the power of social drinking, that we cannot
refrain from giving it. A man who had been a drunkard
for several years, two years before the war, reformed and
remained true to his pledge. When the call for troops
came, he enlisted, and served his country faithfully; and
at the close of three years, re-enlisted for the war, and
received a furlough for thirty days, and started for his
home. He arrived within about a mile of his house, and
met some old friends; and one of them invited him to
rest at his house before going home. He reluctantly
accepted, and while resting there, the lady of the house
brought in a glass of home-made wine. He of course
refused, saying that he had not drank anything, and
would rather be excused. She said, "It is nothing but
wine of our *own make*, and would not harm a child."
Under her advice he took the fatal cup. It revived a
slumbering appetite, and from this place he went to a
rum-shop, and drank to such an extent as to make him
almost crazy. And, strange to say, he met his wife, whom
he had not seen for three long years, with a blow, that
caused her death in a few days; and we have looked
upon this man working at hard labor, inside the walls of
a prison which is to be his home for life. This is no
fancy sketch, but an awful reality.

The following letter was found among some old papers,
and shows better than any words or incidents we can
present, how hard Uniac struggled years before he
signed the pledge at Camp Convalescent. We give it in
full.

NEW YORK, 18—.

MY DEAR FRIEND: — You and I have passed through many scenes in life together, — some pleasant to remember, and some we would gladly forget.

My head aches, and my hand trembles this morning; while my heart is very sad.   After I left you last night, I managed to get home, and went to bed, and fell into a heavy slumber.   On waking, I found myself very weak and sick, and began to meditate on the way we are wasting our lives, throwing away all the grand opportunities that are opening up to the young men of this sublime age; and I thought I would immediately write, and implore you to commence with me, this very night, the fight with our appetite.

I tell you, my dear fellow, all who love us will help us.   God will help us also, if we only help ourselves.   Now will you meet me this evening, say at the sunset hour, and as the god of day sinks to rest, let us take each other by the hand, and solemnly promise that henceforth we *will* be free men.   I know the struggle will be a hard one. I have tried it, and I have failed; but we will remember "in the bright lexicon of youth there is no such word as fail."   Though I feel weak physically, I never felt stronger in my purpose to relieve myself from this power which has been my life's bane, and I hope you will also feel the importance of taking this step *now*, before it is too late.   It will be harder next week, than now.   In God's name, let us begin.   I have learned to respect and love you; you have been one of my dearest friends, and I am anxious for your future welfare.   I noticed the anxious look on your mother's face when I called for you last night; and, how tenderly did she say, "Now do come in early, and be very careful where you go, and what you do." Do you remember?   I hope you will start with me, for it will make me stronger if you begin at the same moment.

Come around and see me before the hour named, if possible.

I met our friend M—— before I began this letter.   I told him how I felt, and the good man took me by the hand, as tears ran down his cheeks, and said, "God help you carry out your noble resolve. You will have my heartfelt prayers."

I feel deeply in earnest about this matter, and beg you will understand my motive for sending this to you.

I will close, hoping to see you to-night.

"Dare to do right,
Dare to be true."

Yours,   UNIAC.

We conclude from this letter, that he had all the time
a keen realization of his own condition, and what his end
must be unless he reformed. We can account for his
repeated attempts to stop in his career, and his repeated
failures, only in the fact, that while his appetite was
strong and powerful, he was not formed by nature in a
way to successfully resist temptations of this character,
for his nature was so social and warm that he would be
defeated in his purpose before he became aware that he
had hardly yielded. He would meet, and be introduced
to some stranger, and, as Mr. Murray says in his letter,
" would seem to break through his reserve, and take his
heart by storm."

We should remember that at this time his associates
were men who used liquor freely; and, no matter how
much he might resolve and re-resolve, the moment he was
in their company he fell.

It is doubtful if there ever was a man who seemed
to desire to reform so earnestly, and still did not accomplish it. His life was one continual struggle. Sometimes, when he had not drank for years, he would come
to his friends, and tell them he was having a hard fight,
and want them to help him.

About the time the letter just referred to was written,
he lost a friend and companion. We find he refers to
it as follows: " A dear friend has been called to his
account, and by this blow we are all reminded of the
importance of living and acting aright; not forgetting
that ' life is real, life is earnest, and the grave is not its
goal.' How much more my dear departed friend might
have accomplished had he not wasted so much of his life

in drinking. Shall I feel this warning, and stop before it is too late?

"Other men have been where I am, and are now honored and loved, because they have conquered themselves. I will try! I do not want it said when I am dead, 'He might have been a good, useful man, but he could not resist his appetite, and died a drunkard.' I will make an effort, and hope I shall succeed! God help me!"

Who can read this letter, and not feel that even at this time he was in earnest in the matter of reforming? By an extract on a piece of paper, we find that he and the young man to whom he wrote, did meet, and began the struggle. We give it here. "Well, J—— and I have started to conquer our enemy. God give us strength to persevere!" And again: "One week has passed, and I have not touched or tasted intoxicating liquors, thank God." And still again: "O, how awful the struggle! My whole system is demanding drink." This struggle did not continue very long, for soon after we read: "Gone is my hope, gone is my resolution, gone is my manhood. I am still a slave to my appetite."

And there was not much hope that his struggle would result in a victory, until circumstances should change around him. Again we are called to say, "The struggle is going on."

In how many hearts is the same kind of a conflict raging, all through the land, God only knows! And while manhood is in danger of being debased and ruined, by being vanquished in the fight, it is the duty of those who are strong to help the weak, tempted soldier

in life's battle, by prayers, influence, kind acts, and gentle words. If you have a flower-garden, you perhaps
have seen the storm beat down your roses, and cause the
beautiful little pinks to droop, and hide their faces,
because of the earth that covers them; and as you have
looked at the garden, you may have said, "My flowers are
ruined"; but with tender hand you have lifted the rose-
bush, and replaced it, in the spot where it used to cling,
to some stronger shrub, and with pure water washed the
faces of the pinks, and rearranged the walks, and have
gone out in the morning, and, behold! the flowers are
blooming more sweetly than ever before. As you have
taken in the fragrance, you perhaps have exclaimed:
" Why, the flowers are all the better for the storm, even
more beautiful than those that have been protected from
winds and rain. So in the world, God's garden, there
are flowers in the shape of noble men and women, who
have been beaten down by the storms of temptation and
sin; and if, with the tender hands of charity, we lift them
up, wash off the blots that sin and crime have left, we
shall behold them blooming with virtues, fairer than many
who have never felt the terrible storm-cloud of temptation beating on their heads. Are the flowers not worth
saving? Are there not gems hidden deep among the
lowlands of life? Go, then, into the by-ways, lift up
and reclaim the fallen, and ye shall not labor in vain,
for, He who rulest the universe hath said, " Ye shall have
your reward."

·CHAPTER V.

DESPAIR OF REFORMING — ENLISTING AS A SOLDIER —
FIRST MONTHS IN ARMY — THRILLING INCIDENTS, ETC.

As nearly all the *real* interest in the life of Uniac gathers round a period of some four or five years, when he was before the public, it will not be necessary to linger much longer over the scenes of his New York life or early days. Those who saw him in his prime, with his eyes flashing and his tongue sending forth eloquent and thrilling words, charming the listener, would not care to have us paint him in the position he occupied about the time the war broke out. Finding no hope for him in the struggle with alcohol, his wife having left him because of drunkenness, when the rebels fired on our flag he said, "I love my adopted country; I do not want to die a drunkard here in the streets of this great city. I will go and fight in defence of liberty, and if I fall, shall at least have a soldier's burial."

He therefore enlisted for three years, in the 88th Regiment N. Y. Volunteers, Co. B. As the company was stationed away from where any liquor was sold, he became sober ; and the captain finding him to be intelligent, and ready to do his duty, appointed him corporal, with the promise of rapid promotion if he would abstain from liquor. In his diary he says, "I was often promoted and as often reduced, from my too great love of the cup."

Army life had a tendency to make him reckless, and he revelled in crime, being sober only when intoxicating liquors were kept from him by army regulations. But he has said that some nights when he was walking guard, he would stop, and resolve never to touch or taste intoxicating liquors again. As he would hear the groans of the sick and wounded, the full force of the danger of dying a drunkard would come upon him, and almost overwhelm him, and he would begin in real earnest the struggle. Every day of his life, almost, he made resolutions to reform and abandon drinking; but they were soon broken.

It may be interesting here to read his record in the United States Army: "Edward H. Uniac, native of Ireland — lawyer. Height, five feet, five inches. Light hair — florid complexion — corporal Co. I, 88th New York Irish Brigade; enlisted Aug. 1861. Since transferred to Co. B. Reduced to the ranks, for having struck an officer while intoxicated."

One fact worthy of especial mention here, that whether in or out of the army, though he sank to the lowest purlieus of drunkenness, mixed and joked with its votaries, yet he was never known to make a practice of using obscene expressions, or take the name of God in vain, with profane intent; he was never in the habit of using tobacco, and had it not been for this inordinate love of liquor, he would doubtless have risen in the army, as he did in civil life, when he was free from it.

For some time before he joined the army he had been

drinking desperately, and after he enlisted he was placed
in quarters where it was almost impossible to get liquor.
The effect was to bring him near the delirium tremens.
He had but ten dollars in the world at this time, and this
he gave for a glass of whiskey, — another proof of the
power of this appetite ! But gradually he overcame this,
and remained for months doing his duty well and
promptly.

In regard to the record of his striking an officer,
alluding to it in his diary, he says : "My temper is not
hasty ; what I have done to merit the court-martial,
I would repeat again on the repetition of the acts that led
to it.   I was court-martialled for committing an act, and
at the same time applauded for committing it."   From
conversations had with him on this point, we judge that
he was partially intoxicated ; and a young lieutenant,
feeling the importance of his shoulder-straps, accosted
him in a rough, ungentlemanlike manner.   Uniac, not
responding to his remarks, he approached, and giving
him a push, said, "Stand out of my way, you drunken
Irishman !"—upon which Uniac turned and struck him
with the back of his hand across the face, and this affair
led to the court-martial, which resulted in his being
reduced to the ranks.   There is nothing remarkable or
worthy of special reference here, regarding his first few
months in the United States service, except to say that it
was one continual struggle and defeat of the man in his
attempts to overcome his appetite.   One day he received
a pass, and visited the hospitals, and while there witnessed
a sad sight that made a deep impression on his mind.
Passing through the wards of one of the largest, he was

accosted by one of the patients, in a weak voice, who requested a glass of water ; and after he had drank a few drops, holding up the tumbler, said, " If I had loved this emblem of purity better, and strong drink less, my system would not have been so wasted and worn as it is to-day." Uniac was deeply interested in what the man had said, and requested him, if he felt strong enough, to tell him something of his life's story. The sick soldier requested to be raised a little, and said, " I was born in the State of New York, of a good family. My boyhood was passed in peaceful pleasure, until I reached the age of seventeen, when I became acquainted with some young men who visited drinking saloons; of course I indulged with them, and you know what followed. Step by step the appetite grew stronger, until I was bound body and soul, and was a disgrace to my friends and myself. The breaking out of the war found me wretched, homeless, and almost friendless. I enlisted, and the exposures and hardships of camp-life were too much for my broken and shattered constitution, and I lie here wasting with consumption, brought on and aggravated by intoxicating drinks."

When he had finished, Uniac felt the man had been telling his own story, with the exception that he was yet spared the fatal disease that had hold of this man. So he told him something of his own career ; and the dying man took his hand in his, and begged of him to stop while he had health and life ; and together, over the goblet of water, they pledged themselves to try to abstain from their life's enemy.

Uniac has often remarked that this scene came before

his eyes in after years when he lifted the cup to his lips.
It was indeed a touching and feeling incident, and it
must have made a deep impression. He never saw
the man again, but took pains to ascertain about him, and
found that he died, and was buried in the National
Cemetery at Arlington. One day after he had signed
the pledge, in company with a friend, he visited this
spot, made sacred by the precious dust of thousands of
the bravest and the best of America's sons ; and as they
wandered through the paths and among the graves of
this consecrated ground, scanning with the deepest
interest the white boards at the head of the mounds, at
the end of one of the long paths they found the grave
they sought, with name and date of death inscribed, and
above that dust they gathered inspiration for the fight
and warfare in behalf of Truth and Temperance. Who
that has wandered there, has retraced his steps without
feeling inspired by his reflective ramblings among the
mounds and monuments of this patriot's resting-place ; and
if the friends of the poor young man who gave the temperance lesson to Uniac in the hospital ever visit that spot,
they must feel a glorious satisfaction in the thought that
a life so nearly wasted as was his, was at last crowned
with a soldier's death and burial ; for a grateful country
will annually strew his grave with sweetest flowers in
memory of his soldier's life and death.

The regiment to which Uniac belonged was a fighting
regiment, and was engaged in some of the most desperate
battles of the war. They had long, weary marches,
and sometimes when Uniac had been trying to be faithful
to his highest convictions of right, and had abstained

from that which had been his greatest curse, it would be after one of these exhausting tramps, that he would yield, if it were possible to procure drink; and in this way passed his first days and months of a soldier's life, marching, tramping, fighting, and struggling. He had a large number of correspondents, and was an interesting letter-writer. He wrote many letters to young people in the vicinity of Boston, encouraging them to labor for the soldiers. One of these letters was received by a Sunday-school scholar, and at a session of the school the letter was read, when it created such an interest that the members soon formed a Soldier's Aid Society, which sent comfort and consolation to many of our brave, wounded, and dying Boys in Blue.

In the following letter, he refers to a movement in the direction of temperance : —

" A movement has been started to induce leading officers of our army to banish liquor from the camps, but it has been done only in a few instances, as the love for it is too great to have it generally adopted."

Many a vacant chair by our firesides was made thus vacant because of blunders committed by men in command of our soldiers while under the influence of liquor. Hundreds of soldiers will testify to the truth of this statement. Who can forget the reports in our newspapers, of some disaster to our arms, concluding with the remark, " Somebody has blundered "? Who does not know the meaning of this? An old soldier, who passed through the war in the capacity of aid or orderly, reported that a prominent officer who had command of a large division, was so much intoxicated on the morning

of an important movement against the enemy, that it was
difficult to understand his directions; and yet this man
had in his charge the lives of the noblest and dearest of
our young men.   Where can we turn in life, and not see
the evils that result from the cup?   When will our nation
turn back this tide of desolation and ruin !   At least we
ought to demand that men, who hold in their hands in
trust the lives of others, whether in the army or in the
walks of civil life, be compelled to abstain from the use
of intoxicating liquors.   Until this is insisted upon, we
cannot take a seat in a railroad car, or a passage on a
steamboat, without the thought coming over us that perhaps the engineer, or some other in a responsible position, may be under the influence of strong drink.   In the
name of hundreds and thousands, slain by men in these
positions, we demand total abstinence as the rule of their
lives.

CHAPTER VI.

SEPARATION FROM WIFE — FINAL LETTER TO WIFE.

DURING the first years of his life as a soldier, his wife applied for a divorce, and it is necessary, for a fair understanding of his situation, to allude to the fact here.

The following beautiful, but sad, letter explains itself, and was the last one he ever wrote to his wife.

"ONCE DEAR ONE, taking a view of the past, with its various changes and strange vicissitudes, its pleasant pictures and sad ones too, I am forcibly struck with two prominent events, which seem to shape and color my past, present, and future. The first was my marriage, the consummation of a love which could not have been more devoted, sincere, and happy. The other is my alienation from my happy and comfortable home, with all its tender and social endearments. These two events meet me, one to console, the other to sadden me. One to build up my hopes and to brighten my future; the other to dash down the edifice, leaving me a miserable wreck, floating past through the desolate ways of the future. A few Christmas eves witnessed the gradual growth and full development of the two events. A few Christmas eves saw the sunniest hopes that ever glowed in human breast chilled with their frosts and buried with their

4

snows, — eves though now silent in the shrouds of the
past, still linger with me, and hourly sweep the sweetest
music o'er the chords of my memory, — eves that brought
sunshine to my soul, from the very chambers of their
icy winters, — eves that will return no more forever.
From the eve of 18—, I date the round of dissipation
that has brought me to my present deplorable situation,
the consequence of which was a separation from my wife
and two little ones.   Our separation was unlooked for.
Our marriage was the realization of a golden dream, a
bright rose from the bud of love; our separation a dark
reality,— the withering of the rose, the crushing of the
bud.   And thus it is that memory wings the pleasant features of the past, and paints its bitter pictures too, while
I silently suffer the stings of bitter remorse, and contemplate the cause of all my difficulty.   This I do in justifi-
cation to myself, for I cannot be justified before the
world.   It knows not the secrets of my heart, and never
will.

"I know I would have acted a more honorable, manly
part, had I walked in a different sphere; but day after
day I was met by companions whose soul centred in
the wine-cup.

"I breathed their baneful influence until I fell, and
when fallen, those who should have counselled, spurned
me, and I resorted to rum to hide my embarrassment
and shame.   It will be urged that that was a weakness,
and serve but to intensify the difficulty.   Granted, but
in so doing, we have to look at the drunkard as a bond-
man; there is not a free fibre in his whole frame; he is
the veriest slave to the basest appetite, nor can effort

of the will, unaided, shake off the fetters that bind him hand and foot, soul and body, all are the slaves of this devouring beverage. We are prone to form too hasty conclusions respecting the drunkard, we do not give due weight to his infirmities, but rather expect him to act as if he was wholly under his own will. He is a man with an immortal spirit that will live as long as yours, one that Christ died to save. . . . I will not weary you. I seek not to justify myself. Friends fled from me; my path was a grim waste, strewn with the debris of family and friends; my days were spent in drinking and hoping for the night. But all is past now; I occupy the lowest strata of humanity, not a friend to cheer me. Even my little daughter will know me but by reputation, and that will make her blush. Oh! the sound of a drunken father's name! Yet amid all this, I sometimes see a brighter future. It is my guardian angel that bids me hope on, while the demon grimly grins despair. With a firm reliance upon the God of all, that I am but fulfilling my destiny, dark and mysterious though it be, I pray that my little one will find in him a father, and that she from whom I am now separated forever, will find in him a husband upon whose arm she may serenely rest, and from whose counsels she may gather wisdom. Yes, M——, you and I will never meet on earth again; still, in my soul, your name and the memory of the past will be sacredly enshrined." . . .

He then speaks of his child, and her future, and seems to be anxious to live in such a manner as not to disgrace her. We have given the above extracts, not to attempt to justify or palliate his course, but to show that he had a keen realization, and, like all men similarly situated, felt at times as though he was neglected by those whom he had reckoned as friends. It is not our purpose to say a single word that shall open or awaken anything that lies in the past, whereby the memory of the dead shall be tainted, or the fair name of the living brought into question. The above letter must have been written after the final separation had taken place. There is a mingling of hope and despair, light and shade, which gives a faint conception of the struggle in which this man was engaged. The hope that he might redeem something that he had lost seemed at times to inspire him. But the veil of sacred love and domestic happiness should not be lifted for us to pry into the motives of either party interested in this affair.

Who can read this sad and tender letter without a pang! As he refers to the resolves he made to lead a different life, and to the evil influence of bad companions causing him to break them, thus carrying misery and sorrow to a happy home, who does not feel the importance of good and pure surroundings for men of this character? — for circumstances do make or unmake a man who is by nature susceptible to every influence that comes in contact. Had this man at this time been encircled by the influence of Christian associations, what might he not have accomplished under God? Let us then purify our cities and towns, by the spreading of correct principles, and many who now stumble will walk erect.

CHAPTER VII.

FIGHTING — WOUNDED — TAKEN PRISONER — LIFE IN
PRISON, ETC.

AMID the din of battle, and novelty of camp life, we
find Uniac, still struggling, now with success, and anon
with defeat. He was promoted often, and in his own
words, as quoted before, "as often reduced, for having
too deeply loved my gin." He was in general battles
at Fair Oaks, Chickahominy, Savage Station, White Oak
Swamp, Gaines' Hill, Bailey's Cross Roads, White House,
Malvern Hill, Antietam, Bull Run, Fredericksburg,
Chancellorville, etc.

He was wounded at Warrington, and afterwards at
Chancellorville, severely, in the third day of the fight.
This occurred by a charge from the 43d Georgia Regi-
·ment. He was entirely helpless, being both wounded
and paralyzed, and in the Adjutant's report was set
down as killed. His comrades left him on the field for
dead, and the rebels began to search for his effects. In
so doing they discovered a Masonic emblem on his
coat, and the lieutenant in command ordered them to
desist.

In a letter he says : —

"He made a close, personal examination of me, and
discovered life in me, after which he had me removed to

a place of safety,   I was conscious of all that was transpiring around me, but could not move nor·articulate a
single sound.   After I became well enough to be moved,
I was sent to Richmond as a prisoner."

His story of his sufferings while in the hands of the
rebels, is familiar to all that are interested in him, and
are thrillingly interesting.   When he went to Richmond,
he weighed one hundred and thirty-eight pounds, and
when he was released, his weight was seventy-eight
pounds.   In a letter to a friend, he says : —

" What I suffered cannot be told, and if told, it would
be hard to believe.   I lived in the very shadow of
starvation."

But had the struggle between the man and his appetite
ceased, among all these changing scenes?   Alas, no ! It
was raging with all of its force and power ; and to show
how strong it was, on one occasion he gave his only vest
and cap to the guard for a glass of whiskey.

Of course his incarceration necessitated an abstinence,
which, coming so suddenly, brought on an attack of
delirium tremens, and a fit of sickness, which reduced
him as stated.   We do not know as his prison life
differed from that of hundreds and thousands of our
brave men, suffering and dying on every hand.   One of
the saddest incidents of breaking a poor fellow's heart
by disappointment, was related by a lieutenant who was
in the prison at the time.   For some reason, the officer
in command seemed to have a desire to avenge himself
on a young officer, and promised him his discharge on a
certain day.   With heart full of hope, he was marched
out with the rest of the prisoners, who were to be dis-

charged, and while all were permitted to go, he was sent back to prison, and another day appointed for his discharge. He wrote on the prison walls, "Disappointed to-day, to be discharged next week"; and so the cruel men led him out week after week, and as often disappointed him; and he kept writing on the wall, "Disappointed. To *be* exchanged"; until he sickened, grew fainter, and the writing on the wall was less bold, and one morning he was missed, and his fellow-prisoners saw, written above all *he* had written, in a bolder hand, these words, "The noble fellow is exchanged at last; earth for Heaven." Such was one of the many ways devised by the wicked ingenuity of the enemies of our country, to torture and make suffer, in every conceivable way, men who had fought and suffered for their flag and country.

Well may a grateful country annually, with solemn music, march to the sacred places where sleep the brave, and strew their resting-places with sweetest flowers, emblematic of purity, gratitude, and patriotism; and shall not the name of Uniac be divested of much of the evil that hung around it during the struggling days with the demon intemperance, from the fact that he was a soldier, suffered, and almost starved, for our country and its liberties?

An incident occurred during Uniac's prison life, which shows the spirit of our soldiers under the most trying difficulties. It was Fourth of July morning, and the prisoners felt patriotic, and resolved to celebrate it as best they might. Uniac was selected to deliver the oration, and had proceeded as far as to say, that

before another Fourth of July rolled around, the rebellion would be crushed, and the tramp, tramp of the
army unlock their prison door, when he was seized by
the guard, and and amidst the chorus of "Hail Colum-
bia" by the whole crowd, carried to a cell in the lower
part of the prison.

Should this prison life, when he comes out of it, also
make him free from the slavery of alcohol, it will
indeed be for his temporal and everlasting welfare.

The terrible scenes he witnessed made a deep impression on his mind.

He saw a brave comrade, who had gone forth under the
same flag, had braved the same dangers, shot down by
the guard, for reaching over the "dead line," so called,
for a small piece of food; and as he held him in his
arms before he died, he looked up into his eyes, and said,
"I have kept the pledge, and die in the faith of my
Maker." These dying words of a comrade who had
been through so many scenes of dissipation with him,
and had reformed and kept his pledge, and died in the
faith of Christ, did much towards Uniac's reformation
in after days.

One day, while in prison, he made an attempt to bribe
the guard, and thereby obtain a glass of liquor. He had
a valuable gold ring that had been given him by a soldier just before he died; and finding he would not procure the drink in any other way, had promised the
guard that if he would procure him a single glass, he
would give him the last five dollars in his possession,
together with the ring. The rebel guard said he would
try and get it to him about dark; and all that day, as he

waited in anticipation of that for which his whole soul
and body seemed to burn, his head began to ache vio-
lently. Before the time came for the soldier to bring
him drink, he was burning up with a fever, and being
unconscious, was taken to a place *called* a hospital, but
in reality a spot of low, damp ground, with here and
there, above the beds of our sick and dying men, torn
and ragged canvas, not enough to shelter them from the
burning rays of the sun, or the pitiless storm. How
long he was unconscious he did not know, but when he
came to awake, he found the sick and dying all around
him; and the power of his appetite was so strong, even
weak as he was, that the first thing he thought of was
the promise of the guard. Looking down at his hands,
he found the ring gone. The guard had stolen it from
him while he slept.

"One night," he said, "as I laid looking up to the
stars, wishing for release even by death, from this dreadful place, the soldier who lay nearest me, called out,
'Comrade, I feel worse; I want some water, my mouth
is burning up. O! for one drop to cool my parched
lips!'" No one was near to help this poor suffering fellow, and he cried till he began to wander in his mind;
and Uniac said it was enough to melt the heart of the
hardest, to hear him talk of his home. Now he would be
talking with his mother, and then with his sister; his
cry grew fainter and fainter; and when the morning
dawned, another brave, starved — yes, worse than starved
— soldier was dead, and another "vacant chair" stood by
some fireside, where those who loved him waited in vain
for him to come "marching home again." Has the story

of the suffering of the boys in blue been overstated?
We may forgive the men who caused the war, but while
patriotism burns on the altar of American hearts, we
cannot forget the terrible wrongs done to the bravest and
best of our young men.

One other instance will show how much was endured
by those brave men, to keep from starving. A young
man had been sick and was recovering, and was very
weak from the need of proper food. He felt the want
of it so much, that he volunteered to go and help bring
water to wash the clothes of the rebel officers. The distance he had to carry the water was so great, that he
struggled and trembled every step he took ; but he was
inspired with the thought that a good meal was promised
those who would do this work. He had brought one
pailful, had got the second, and started to return with it,
but was not strong enough, and stopped to rest a moment,
when he was ordered to move on by the guard ; but not
being able to obey promptly, was shot on the spot by
the man in charge of the squad.

It is difficult to believe it possible for men professing
to be Christians, and living in the light of this glorious
age, to be so cruel and heartless ; but we have had too
much evidence from eye-witnesses, yes, from those who
felt the worst that has been told, to doubt it for a single
moment. Many of these scenes Uniac saw and felt, and
he resolved if he came out of this living tomb alive, to
tell to the people of the North the horrors of the rebellion. This.promise he kept, and during the presidential
campaign of 1864, did great service for the Union, by
telling the voters what the soldiers had suffered, and

appealed to them to stand by them and the government, in its effort to crush out and punish those men, who had insulted the flag and murdered their brothers.

It is not necessary to dwell much longer on what he did and saw at these prisons. Suffice it to say, that he here gathered an experience which in after life was of service to him and the cause of the Union.

In the following he gives us his feelings and struggles. "O, my dear friend, I cannot begin to express on paper, or with the tongue, the awful suffering of the rebel prisons. When I think how much God permitted me to pass through, and to escape at last with my life, I feel to praise and thank His holy name. And then it seems hardly possible, that amid all the suffering I never lost my appetite or desire for liquor. I remember I used to have days when it would seem as though I would give my right arm for a glass of whiskey. I have walked my prison floor like a caged tiger.

"O, sir! my struggle was indeed fearful. And then, when by sickness I was so much reduced that I was hardly able to lift my head from the pillow, still I would often pant for my beverage. My struggle is fearful, and I do not feel that in any position I am safe."

What a testimony is this letter in favor of the principle of total abstinence; for here was a man, while in prison, while sick, while sober, in all kinds of the most trying circumstances, never free from the appetite he had formed for strong drink. Let this man who speaks from bitter experience be heeded and listened to by all who are in danger of forming the accursed habit.

Who can afford to run the risk of placing himself

under the power of such a tyrant as a depraved appetite
becomes? Were there no other instance in all history
but this story of Uniac's struggle, the bare possibility of
becoming like this ought to be enough to prevent any
man who values his manhood and freedom from ever
"touching or tasting" that which may make him a slave
of the meanest kind.

CHAPTER VIII.

RELEASE FROM PRISON — SIGNING THE PLEDGE — LETTER FROM JOHN B. GOUGH — WORK IN THE CHRISTIAN COMMISSION — THRILLING LETTERS FROM THE BATTLE-FIELD, ETC.

AFTER remaining in prison six months, he was exchanged, and was in a very weak condition, only weighing about eighty pounds. He said, "As weak as I was, when we caught sight of the old flag, I joined with my comrades in giving it three hearty cheers." He was sent to "Camp Distribution," to remain there until he should become strong enough to join his regiment. Soon after coming to this place, he began a correspondence with Mr. W—— Keith's family, of Boston, and it will be seen from what follows, that it resulted in a dear friendship, lasting till his death. Without giving further incidents of some of his desperate drinking spells, we will proceed to speak of what must be more pleasant to the reader, and that is his signing the pledge. Through the kindness of John B. Gough, Esq., we are enabled to give this in Mr. Gough's own language.

"MY DEAR SIR, — On the 16th of January, 1864, I was invited by Mr. Ballantyne and other gentlemen of Washington, to deliver two addresses to the soldiers at Camp Distribution. During the morning lecture, I noticed a

man seated directly in front of me, whose eyes were
intently fixed on me ; not a smile passed over his face,
but he had an earnest look that attracted me to him.
His hair was matted, a dirty rag was bound about his
head, his eye was blood-shot, his face bloated, and his
whole appearance spoke of utter neglect. Being interested in his apparent abandonment, I inquired of an
officer who he was. He said, he is the worst man in the
company and the most brilliant, but is so given to intemperance, that nothing but a miracle can save him. In the
afternoon he was present in the same place and the same
condition, and as earnest in his attention as before. At
the close of my speech, the soldiers were invited to sign
the pledge ; he came forward and affixed his name.

"My wife was standing near, and offering her hand to
him, said, ' God help you to keep it.' He replied,
' Thank you, madam, I will remember that.'

"I spoke a few words of encouragement, shook hands
with him, and saw him no more till nine months after,
when, on the occasion of a lecture in Philadelphia, Mr.
George H. Stewart said to me, 'There is a friend of
yours waiting to see you in the committee room.' Uniac,
not the Uniac of a few months back, but Uniac the man,
Uniac the gentleman, grasped me with both hands. Our
meeting was very delightful to me ; we had quite a talk,
and I was touched by his evident manifestation of affection.

"Some time after, he was an inmate of my family for
about a week, and we all became much attached to him.

"I saw him but seldom, but we always met as dear
friends.

"I can hardly tell you how shocked I was when the news came to us, 'Uniac has fallen.' You and many of his friends in Boston know better than I his mighty struggles, and their efforts to save him. I send you three letters, which you may use as you please."

We have given all Mr. Gough wrote under this head, as we could not well divide the part that refers to his signing the pledge, and that which speaks of his fall.

Mr. Uniac always spoke of Mr. Gough as one of his dearest friends, and in his hour of sorest need there was no one who did more for him than he under whose influence he signed the pledge. Uniac used often to allude to the hour when he sat listening to the eloquent and thrilling words at Camp Distribution; he said, when he heard that Mr. Gough was to speak to the soldiers, the thought flashed across his mind, "Perhaps I may be assisted in my struggle with my appetite, if I attend." He was in the terrible condition described above; and as he went towards the place where the meeting was to be held, he met a squad of soldiers, and one of them jeeringly remarked, "There goes a good subject for Gough's lecture." These words cut Uniac to the quick, and he thought to himself, "Is it possible? Have I sunk so low in the scale of humanity, as to be pointed at by my companions in crime? By God's help, I will try to be a man once more."

The morning speech gave him much to think of; and among the many good words spoken, he said, while looking intently at the speaker, he seemed to catch his eye. Gough was in the midst of one of his most powerful appeals, when, pointing his finger almost directly at

Uniac, he said, "You can be a man; you have an
immortal spirit beating in your bosom, which must live
forever. Will you try? God will help you, good angels
will help you, the prayers of God's people will help you,
and you will be successful in the struggle." These words
thrilled· him, and the sun of hope shone as he had not
seen it for months; and in the afternoon, when he had
put his name to the pledge, and turned to come away,
and heard the words, "God help you to keep it," spoken
by Mrs. Gough, he felt strong in his purpose to try, and
he began the contest in real earnest; but how terrible
the fight, God, and those who have passed through some
such experience, only know.

We give a few extracts from his diary written at this
time.

"1864, January 19th. Took the pledge.

"20th. Well, another day has passed over my head,
and I feel that it has but added just so much strength to
my resolution to keep my pledge inviolate against all
influences from without or within.

"21st. Still another day added to the calendar of my
sober life, and O ! how much I need each day, for how
unevenly cast are the balance sheets of my life ! Eleven
of my best years spent in drunken dissipation !

"22d. What a frail thing is human nature after all !
How weak and helpless when left alone. How fruitless
in the hour of adversity. How prone to call on friends
for aid and counsel, when they, under similar circumstances, are quite as frail as we. How seldom we apply
to the proper source of peace, for that sweet rest which
Christ alone can give ! Why is it that I have lived so

long, and never realized this fact until the last few days?

"Why have I overlooked so beautiful a truth? Had I believed it sooner, what a world of misery it would have saved me, as I struggled against the tide of fate that seemed to have directed its whole force against me. It would have soothed me in my hours of solitary anguish. But those days are passed, and I am spared to partake of the future, with all its sunny hopes, in the love of my Redeemer and my God.

"26th. 'The light of the wicked shall be put out.' The truth of this text I know and can verify. I have walked for years in darkness, without one single ray to light my pathway of sin and crime. There was a time when I walked in the light, when the songs of birds were hymns of praise, and the winds sighed the love and greatness of God. Mine was then the peaceful path of innocent childhood. I had a mother to direct me into the paths of piety. I had a Christian father, and every Sunday found me at the foot of the altar, filling up my young soul with divine truth and love. My light shone then; my hopes bounded from each crag of life into a smooth and lovely plain, and frisked and frolicked like an uncaged bird on a bough of the blooming orange-tree; my faith looked over aloft, and beheld with unerring certainty a radiant home awaiting me, in the cloudless presence of my God.

"But how sad the change! Left alone at fifteen, I soon fell into the ways and wickedness of the world. I followed its luring phantoms until my light was extinguished, and I groped amid the dark debris, to find my way only to places of still deeper darkness.

5

"In vain I teased philosophy; in vain I sought reason
to restore me to the happy frame of mind that I had once
experienced. They led me from dream to dream, each
becoming the more vague, the more I resolved it. The
present was dark indeed; the future looked no brighter.
Now came in upon me Doubt, with her twin companion,
Believe-nothing, and both took full possession of my
soul, and froze it with their icy touch. The earth was
silent; she did not speak to me through the little flower
as she had of yore.

"The trees were dumb. Birds sang the song of despair, and each root and fibre of the gnarled forest trees
spoke to me only of wreck and woe."

In other extracts and letters, we shall see that he had
no sooner placed his feet firmly on the rock of temperance, than he began to feel the importance of doing all
in his power to save those friends and companions around
him, who were in danger from the same cause that had
bound him for so many years. It is a good test of the
sincerity of a converted man to see him anxious for the
welfare of others.

We now find him a changed man, well-dressed, clean,
good-looking, polite, and hopeful. But a few weeks ago,
and he was in the condition in which Gough found him.
O! how much it will do for a man to control a depraved
appetite. Now Uniac is on the threshold of a new life,
with new hopes and resolves, but the battle is not
ended. No! it has just begun with real firmness. And
how hard must he fight for his virtue and manhood!
How many times will he find the enemy almost too strong
for him to stand up against!

It will be only by faith in God, and a determined purpose, that he will be able to conquer in this war.

Soon after signing the pledge, he labored in the work of the Christian Commission. And the gentlemen who were with him in this field of labor bear testimony to the transformation he had undergone, and to his fidelity and the desire to help the suffering wherever he could find them. Mr. Geo. H. Stewart of Philadelphia, well known in connection with this Commission, who was one of his kindest and best friends at this time, speaks in the highest terms of the work Uniac did, especially of his labors for the victims of intemperance. He worked night and day, often saying, " How much strength do I get in trying to help some poor fellow to stand." He continued to follow the army, fighting when able, or detailed to work with the Commission, in the care of the wounded.

The following beautifully descriptive letters were written to friends in the vicinity of Boston : —

" We took up quarters here yesterday morning, and right glad were we to have some time for rest in prospect.

" Our march has been very severe, and several of our party have given out ; indeed, out of the original ten who started, three only remain of it for active service ; namely, Mr. Chase, Mr. Snow of Andover, and myself.

" But if the marching was severe, the glory was really compensating.

" Imagine yourself walking one whole day and night without sleep or rest, except sufficient time to prepare coffee and hard tack. Then you have about five hours sleep, and you are marched thirty miles again ; when you are brought to a sudden stand by the booming of cannon, and the quick crash of musketry.

"Time is momentous. Its pendulum at each stroke ticks out the life from some patriot's breast, and shell and shot punctuates his fall. You forget the last weary march, you hold your breath in awful agony. The noise grows louder and louder: from the lines of the enemy may be heard the shouts of victory. Your lines are broken, and the cavalry are flying through the woods in all directions, from the well-directed fire of a superior (in numbers) force.

"The day is lost, and your brave have fallen in vain. You begin to feel the effects of your march now, you are foot-sore, and, worse, you are heart-sore indeed.

"Suddenly a wild cheer bursts in from the left, followed by a wilder roll of musketry. You dash through the woods, your heart tells you that the cheer is friendly to your cause.

"'T is the 5th and 24th corps in hot pursuit of the rebs. You press on, and in a few hours you see the American flag, planted in an open field, and the confederate rag dipping obedience to it. Are you heart-sore now? Louder are the foe. Grant holds their lives in the silence of the moment. In that well-charged three hundred and eighty pieces of cannon is certain death to every man, unless they surrender to our victorious army to-day, and complete that surrender before four o'clock, P. M. Lee and Johnson, Gordon and Picket, Longstreet and Ewell, ay, the whole army of Virginia are here, and what is better, they are also helpless.

"O! I would not have missed this sight for all the

sights that I have ever seen. I have passed over some very delightful country. Many of the trees bear beautiful blossoms, and every species of the violet blooms here to perfection.

"I enclose you a few stems and leaves, gathered on the last battle-field, and where the treaty was consummated.

"I have not heard from any of my correspondents for the last two weeks. I have been cut loose from civilization during that time, but I am in the hopes of reaching City Point in a few days."

The following was written after he had smoothed the dying brow of a soldier who spoke of home, and is touchingly beautiful : —

"There is a sunshine in the very word home. When the heart is sad, when its silent portals are closed to pleasure from without or from within, the sweet word home will melt the seal and admit the sunshine.

"Why has home so many endearments, so many sacred charms, so many tender remembrances found in no other place? It is because the heart's purest tendrils are linked around it, and the soul's sweetest interests are blended with those who constitute it and make it, and give it its endearing name.

"God intended that home should be a hallowed spot, a type of the place of eternal rest. 'Home is where the heart is.' Hearts are dust, but while they beat they have hopes and loves. Those hopes and loves, while the heart beats, should encircle the home ; and when the heart beats not, should go up to the home built by the father's hands.

'Hearts are dust, heart's loves remains,
Heart's loves, will meet thee again.'

"If the spirits of the loved dead have any share in the cares and concerns of those who were dear to them in this brief life, how joyful they must feel when they see them bending their feet in the ways of God, and leading lives that will secure them an inheritance and a crown.

"Let bright hopes be yours. Make each hope a jewel; let your daily labor brighten them. Set them in a prayerful heart. God will gather them up at last, re-set them, and invest them with celestial brilliancy.

"I will try to meet you and greet you when you wear your crown."

"On Friday night I spoke at Warren Station, where I remained that night.

"At half-past three in the morning I was aroused by the sound of battle.

"I rode to the scene of action and back to Humphrey's Station, which is the nearest R. R. Station to this C. C. Station, from which I am now addressing you. When I arrived, all was quiet, and continued so until one P. M., when the firing began slowly on the left of the 2d corps.

"It developed itself gradually until about three, when the whole line in front of the 2d corps opened with fearful rapidity, and so continued until half-past seven P. M., when it ceased at once on both sides as if by mutual consent. I stood under the fire all day, indeed so did all of our delegates, and many a wounded soldier was relieved by us.

"When the firing had ceased, we advanced over the breastworks, and went out among the dead and wounded who lay on the field uncared for.

"The first person I came across was a Capt. Smith, of Co. D, 64th N. Y. He was shot through the knee, and died from the loss of blood. I cut a lock of his hair, registered his name, took charge of his few effects, and pushed forwards. During this time I am accompanied by Dr. Patterson of Philadelphia, whose heart seems deeply moved by the solemnity of the scene. He will write to the captain's family.

"I next met a little boy. He belongs to the 16th Michigan. He dies while I am rendering him all the assistance I can.

"Many and sad were the scenes I witnessed.

"I returned towards the field hospital, which was in a farm-house that in the morning was held by the rebels. On my way I met Generals Miles and Bartlett. I gave them some refreshment, which they sadly needed. Miles has a boy twelve years of age on his staff. He ranks a second lieutenant. He knows no danger.

"The loss in the 5th corps has been small. In fact our total loss is small, considering the *heavy fighting*, but the wounded are very badly wounded indeed. Several men are shot right through the stomach and breast. Their suffering is fearful. Death to them would be a welcome messenger.

"CITY POINT, VA.

"By the caption of my letter you see where I am. At noon to-day I leave for Hatch's Run. This trip may not have been a prudent one, as weak as I am, but I hope it may prove profitable. There are reasons why I should come, however. Among them, none so pungent as the

fact that the army may soon move, and I felt compelled
to address them for a short time, before they broke up
their winter quarters. I will not remain long, however,
and as soon as I return I am off for Boston.

"This struggle between love of friends, and duty to
God, is often desperate; but duty to God should prevail.

"I reached Washington on the eve of the 3d, and witnessed the President's Inauguration. There was nothing
to prevent it from being the greatest scene ever witnessed
in this country, except the speech of Johnson, the vice-
president elect. It was said that he was drunk. His
speech gave one reason to believe it.

"I left Washington on the 8th, and reached here yesterday, at half-past two P. M. The scenery of the Potomac cannot compare with the Delaware or Hudson. The
James, however, is so pregnant with historic interest, so
woven with the struggles through which the nation is
passing, and from which, like Crisites from the blood of
Medusa, it will emerge into a golden life.

"There stand the ruins of Jamestown, the oldest settlement of Virginia; and there, in the centre of its
scarcely perceptible ruins, a small pillar; it is the corner
of the church where Pocahontas was baptized. O! what
fearful work war has done along the banks of this river,
as well as through the whole State. The stripes laid
along the sun-tipped hills, and the scars which mar her
pleasant vales, will remain there to remind many genera-
tions of the utter madness of secession.

"The punishment inflicted on this State has been dreadful, — retributive, but just. Her King Cotton, with his
robes of human slavery, has lost his crown and sceptre

forever, and the black man, the dusky jewel chained to
his crown, has been torn from it, and is now being bright-
ened and recut, by the lapidaries of the gospel, to be
placed henceforth and forever in the diadem of Jesus.

"Great, very great are the works of the Lord.

"You may hear the question often asked, 'Why don't
Grant move?' For the simple reason that it is wholly
impossible. This country is in a dreadful condition; the
ambulances and train wheels are up to the axles in mud.

"This whole country is familiar to me. I stood upon
the very spot, last evening, where the rebels laid me,
previous to delivering me to the Union forces, at the time
of my parole.

"But O what a change! Then the fields were green,
and the trees interlaced each other above the long avenue
leading to the wharf; and as I lay helpless then, even
in my thraldom I could enjoy a kiss from the red lips of
the sun, as they trembled through the leaves; and yet
I love the change, though the whole face of nature wears
a dismal shade, and the sun is hid in clouds, while now
and then he wreaks his vengeance on said clouds,
by melting them into copious showers. I love the
change, because the banner that I have sworn to defend
floats here unmolested, and brightens into liberty the
darkest clouds.

"Will you remember me in sweet kindness to all, and
pray for me very often; and believe me that my heart
and affections are with you all, at all times."

If this man had been touched by some magic wand,
and in an instant transformed into a new being, he could
not have appeared more changed than these letters show

him to be. Not only has the outer man undergone a transformation, but his heart has been baptized with new purity and heavenly love. His victory over his appetite has inscribed manhood on his brow, and as a servant of God he has gone into the harvest-field to labor.

If on every street corner there was not temptation held out to him, he might walk unharmed through all his future; but while our streets echo to the voice of dissipation, and the very air is pregnant with the intoxicating element, hope for the safety of this man, and men like him, is faint. Which shall the law protect, our homes and brothers, or the rum traffic?

This is a question of profound interest to this age, and we must meet it, and settle the right, or our nation will be a nation of helpless drunkards. "I would give half of my princely fortune," says a merchant of New York, "if I had the power to pass a liquor-shop."

"O, my God, give me strength of will and purpose to go from my work to my home, without entering a rum-shop," says a poor weak mechanic on his bended knees, as great beads of sweat stand out on his forehead. And so are hundreds, from burdened hearts, crying to-day. What is there left for us to do for these men? Nothing but by the strong arm of the law to sweep from their path these pitfalls; and God hasten the day when the people of our country shall awake to this duty, and by the logic of votes, convince those upon whom every other argument has failed.

CHAPTER IX.

DESPERATE STRUGGLE WITH APPETITE — THRILLING STORY.

UNIAC still stands, for now we find him accepting invitations to speak for temperance, and thus gaining strength to resist the temptations that beset him on every side, in and around Washington. In his diary we find, "Jan. 29," the following: "I spoke at the Marshall House in Alexandria, and afterwards sat down to a sumptuous supper. We had a large party, and some very distinguished men, — among them Senator Mac-Dougall, of California. Liquor flowed freely, but thank God I came from that room the victor over my appetite. My sky of life grows brighter, the light is shining all the time. I now see the silver lining to the clouds through which I have passed; my life shall be devoted to God and humanity." At this time however, there would be periods when it would seem as though he must yield, — and he would do all in his power to stand. He would often take long walks, and try to find something to divert his mind, and change the current of his thought.

One evening he was in the city of Washington, still fighting with his old enemy, debating whether to yield or not. He was still a soldier, and having a pass from his comrades, he wandered over the National Ceme-

tery in Arlington, saying to himself, perhaps it will help
me to take a reflective wandering among the mounds
and monuments of this consecrated spot, where sleep so
many of the brave who fell fighting for flag and country.

He walked through the avenue regularly laid out, on
either side of which rises the plain slab upon which is
inscribed the name and regiment of the buried soldier;
surely a place to gain inspiration for the battles of life.
Near the end of one of the longest avenues, he stopped
beside a grave that had been recently strewn with sweetest flowers; everything about it looked as though some
loving hand had carefully and tenderly beautified it. On
the plain white board, written by a fair hand, was the
following : —

"Sleep, noble heart! for when thou wast among us, or
on the battle-plain, thou didst contend and fight, how
hard none but God and you can tell; but you died, thank
God, victor over thy terrible enemy, rum; and one that
loves thee, records it as the grandest epitaph that can be
inscribed above thy resting-place." And beneath this
the lady had signed her name.

He said, as he read these touching words, the tears
ran down his cheeks, and he returned to Washington a
stronger man, resolving to fight and conquer as had the
noble fellow of whom he had just read; but alas, he did
not know the strength of the enemy with which he had to
deal.

He thought much of the inscription he had read, and
resolved to write to the lady, and tell her his story, and
ask her more of the man, above whose grave he had stood
at Arlington. He wrote, and after waiting several weeks,
received the following sad but beautiful letter.

WISCONSIN, ——, 18—.

DEAR SOLDIER, — Your kind letter was received some days ago, and I embrace the first opportunity that presents itself to reply. The grave that you say you wept above, was my only brother's, noble, gifted, and unfortunate. I, his only sister, grew up with him, and O! sir, how much I loved him, none can tell. We played together, and wandered through the green fields by day, and at evening when the stars had come out, with father and mother we gathered around the fireside, and our dear boy talked of his future, and of what he hoped to accomplish in the world, until I almost longed to be a man, that I might share with him his trials and victories. We never thought of sorrow or trouble, for our future was cloudless. but O! dear soldier, we had our dark days all too soon. As we grew older,. a neighbor of ours began the manufacture of domestic wines, and from the first lot they made, brought a few bottles to our home. They little knew what they were bringing to that peaceful home. We all drank, but my brother seemed to love it; and you know the rest, he went from this to stronger drink for years, until the appetite bound him hand and foot. I will not repeat what he and I suffered in the struggle to have him relieved from the curse. One night, after one of his terrible drinking spells, taking my hand he said, "By God's help, I never will touch or taste the accursed drink again;" and in the quiet of that autumn evening we knelt and prayed God for strength.

He kept his pledge, and when the war broke out enlisted; for, he said, perhaps my old enemy may attack me again, and I cannot better die than for my country. He marched away, and his letters were full of hope and promise, and each one closed by saying, "It is a severe struggle, but I keep my pledge." One morning news came to us that he was badly wounded. I hastened to the hospital, and held him in my arms, and just before he died he said, "I thank God I have conquered rum."

As I wrote what you read on his tombstone, and arranged the flowers on his grave, tears fell thick and fast, but my heart gratefully thanked God that he died a sober man, a noble death for a noble cause; and may you gather encouragement and hope from his successful struggle and glorious death. God bless and keep you is the wish of

Yours very truly,

M—— G——.

Where shall we look in all history for a brighter example of true heroism. He not only fought bravely on the battle-field, but he conquered the enemy within him. Who shall say his reward is not that of those to whom is said, "Well done, good and faithful servant, enter thou in"? for surely he had kept the faith, and there must have been a crown of glory awaiting him.

We should not too harshly judge these poor diseased men, for they are not only sick in body, but have "a mind diseased."

Some contend that there is too much sympathy for these "slaves of appetite," but when we read a story like the above, as well as when we trace the struggles of Uniac, how is it possible for us to pity too much?

A soldier who had often gained promotion for his gallantry on the field of battle, lay one night on his bed, raving like a madman, crying for some one to give him "rum." His wife bent over him with the most tender solicitude. When sober, he loved her dearly ; but now, because he thought she had taken his liquor away,— when the attention of all present was turned in some other direction,— he turned on her, and with a blow felled her to the floor. After he had done it, he seemed to become for a moment sober, and he cried out, " O my God ! I have killed my best friend." We lifted her up, and soon restored her to consciousness. He watched us, and, when she revived, he took her hand, and said, " Why did I strike her? All because I wanted this liquor. O ! what will a man not do for the accursed stuff !" And, as through the long night we watched with a man we knew was noble and generous when free from the evils of liquor, but now, ready to sacrifice his best friend, we felt that he needed sympathy, for he would not put himself in this condition willingly.

If this, that men put into their mouths to steal away their brains, is so dreadful in its final results, what young man can even afford to run the chance of touching or tasting it, in any form or shape.

Uniac had a kind heart, and took a deep interest in any one who was in trouble or want, and was ready and willing to share the last cent with them. He would often take a long walk to see if he could not do good to some one in trouble. He would call these his manhood-making walks, for he used often to say how much better a man feels if he can only do some good.

No man had a keener appreciation of what constitutes true politeness. He also loved adventures, and this trait in his character he found opportunity to satisfy.

One day he was wandering about Washington, trying to keep back the desire that was more than usually pressing in its demands for him to yield, when he met a little girl crying bitterly. He stopped her, asked her what the matter was, and found that her father and mother had sent her out to buy some rum, that she had lost the money given her to pay for it, and she knew if she went back without the liquor or money, she would receive severe treatment; and she was crying as though her little heart would break.

Uniac took her by the hand, and asked her to show him her home, promising to protect her. She led him to the outskirts of the city, and turned into the door of a miserable-looking hut, and, going up into the attic,

opened a door.   Inside lay a woman, ragged and dirty,
while in an old chair sat a bloated-looking man.   The
moment the child opened the door, he greeted her with
an awful oath, and asked her where she had been so long ;
but seeing Uniac, he stopped, and after surveying him
from head to foot, inquired what he wanted.   Uniac told
him he had come to try and help him and his little one.

The woman on the bed seemed to hear these words,
for she opened her eyes and made some remarks, at the
same time shaking her finger at the child, as much as to
say, " Wait till this man has gone."

After talking kindly to the man, telling him the story
of his own life, he succeeded in getting his attention, and
what he said about the possibility of his becoming a man
once more seemed to touch his heart, and tears ran
thick and fast down his cheeks.   Then opening his arms,
he cried, " Come to me, my dear little one ; God knows
I would not injure or disgrace you, were it not for
rum."

After he had somewhat controlled himself, he told
Uniac his life's story, briefly as follows : —

" I was born in Massachusetts ; my parents were mov-
ing in the best society.   I had two brothers and one
sister.   Our home was one of the pleasantest, and the
future was all golden with hope, when the " gold fever "
broke out.   I, with many others, contracted it, and
being about twenty-one years of age, I thought this
would be a good way to start in life ; and so my oldest
brother and myself left those we loved, and took passage for the ' Golden State.'   I had then only drank

occasionally cider, and felt not the least danger from intemperance. I had attended one or two temperance meetings, held in my native town, but had been in the habit of regarding temperance lecturers as an unreasonable class of men, and thought it was only fools who became drunkards.

"We arrived in California in good condition, and immediately set out for the gold diggings. We had a little money, and invested in a land claim in a settlement of miners, where we soon began life in real earnest. There was a trader in the place, who supplied the wants of the men, with what was necessary as well as what was a curse to many, and of no real benefit to any one, as I have since learned by bitter experience. The first few weeks we worked there, we were quite fortunate in our digging, and succeeded in making quite a fair amount of money. My brother as well as myself was in the habit of spending the evenings at the store, and often drank. We did this for some time before we began to feel any bad effects from the same, but soon my brother began to neglect his work, and would come to our hut late at night, badly intoxicated. I also grew worse and worse, till we had lost nearly everything we had called our own. One night my brother, from excessive drinking, was taken sick, and I stood beside him and heard him cry for drink, and I had not the power to give it to him. A burning fever took possession of him, and for two weeks I watched him sink away. Not once did he know me, but raved, and often talked of mother and home, till the tears would run down my cheeks in streams. I was unable to supply his wants, and one

6

night I held him in my arms, and just before midnight he
opened his once beautiful blue eyes, and looking up into
mine, said, 'George, where am I? Where is mother
and sister? All is calm, I hear music.' His head fell
back, and he was dead.

"With my own hands I made him a grave, and planted
flowers above it; and the evening I buried him, I kneeled
beside that sacred spot, and asked God to help me to
abstain forever from the use of intoxicating liquors. I
wrote the sad news home, and asked them to send me
money enough to come back to them. I left him I loved,
and he sleeps to-night in a distant part of the land, with
no stone to mark the spot where I laid him, unknown
and forgotten. except by those who loved him, far away
from where he rests.

"I went back to my native town, began business, pros-
pered, became acquainted with a beautiful girl, — there
she lays, you would hardly think it was the same one, —
we were married. All of the circle in which she moved
drank wine, and it was not long before I yielded, and it
is the same old story over again; I not only sank back
again, but, worse than all, she I loved went also. We
have been from bad to worse, till at last I got a chance
here, but I was turned off six months ago, and here we
are, as you find us, — wretched and miserable, and the
future of our child darkened. What shall we do to
reform? Is there hope," he cried as he finished, "for
her and for me?"

What could be the effect of such a story on a man
like Uniac? Of course it made him stronger, and he
said, "I feel as though there was a Providence in my

meeting this little child, for I was in the midst of a desperate struggle, and this story helped me to stand." He, by the aid of some gentlemen interested in the temperance question, succeeded in doing something for the family, and had the satisfaction of seeing the man and wife both sign the pledge. The evening of the day he met the little girl, he wrote the following : —

Sad is the drunkard's life,
  Wasting in crime,
Far from the path of right,
  Reckless of time.
Tears of repentant grief
  Chill as they start,
Hardly a tender thought
  Wake in his heart.

Often a single spark
  Kindles a flame,
Kindness may win him back,
  Prayers may reclaim.
Go where he sits alone,
  Burdened with care,
Tell him his sinful course,
  Plead with him there.

Picture a happy past
  Gone from his sight,
Bring back his early youth,
  Cloudless and bright.
Tell how a mother's eye
  Watched while he slept,
Tell how she prayed for him,
  Sorrowed and wept.

Point to the better land,
  Home of the blest;
Where she has passed away,
  Gone to her rest.

O'er that departed one
Memory will yearn,
God, in his mercy, grant
He may return.

We have such information as to lead us to feel sure
that the subjects of these incidents are correct to the
letter; and they are but the counterparts of similar ones
all over our country. Let us raise up the banner of
total abstinence and bid all come under its folds. Lift
up the fallen, throw the cords of sympathy around the
weak and tempted. Let manhood be written on the
brow of the most degraded. Let us help the struggling
hearts, and we shall have our reward, though it may not
come during this life; but just over the river crowns
await those who labor for humanity and God.

" It may not be our lot to wield
  The sickle, in the ripened field;
  Nor ours to hear on summer's eves
  The Reaper's song among the sheaves;
  But ours the grateful service, whence
  Comes day by day the recompense,
  The hope, the purpose staid,
  The fountain, and the noon-day shade.
  And were this life its utmost span,
  The only end and aim of man,
  Better the toil in fields like these,
  Than waking dreams, and slothful ease.
  Our lives, though falling like our grain,
  Like that revives and lives again;
  And early called, how blest are they
  Who wait in Heaven the Harvest day ! "

CHAPTER X.

A SHORT time after he had signed the pledge, and
hardly knew whether he or his appetite was to win the
victory, a prominent officer in the army invited him to
attend a military supper given in honor of a victory of
the Union arms. He told me that he debated long and
well in his mind the question whether to attend or not.
He said "he knew wine and other intoxicating drinks
would flow as freely as water, and he doubted his power
to withstand the temptation." However, by the persua-
sions of friends, he consented to go; and he afterwards
said that if he ever prayed God for strength, it was
as he entered that hall.   He found at the festive board
his friends and companions, and, as he had thought, his
old enemy — wine. Speeches were made, and all in the
room drank the sentiments in the liquor but himself.
The chairman noticed it, and called on him for a toast,
and offered to pledge his health in a glass of wine.   He
said for a moment he faltered, when strength returned
to him. He arose from his chair, filled a glass with

sparkling water, **and** said, " Mr. Chairman : With pleasure will I drink your health, but it must be in cold water."

The attention **of the** whole company was riveted on him, and the most profound silence prevailed as he slowly lifted his glass in his hand, and impressively pointing to it, gave the following beautiful and eloquent tribute to cold water : —

" I took up the glass, I filled it with water, I held it up between me and the light, while that wondrous agent kept shooting prismatic arrows through the liquid drops. I compared it with the wine in my neighbor's glass, and the wine lost by the comparison. I compared it with yonder goblet of champagne, foaming, fretting, sparkling for a moment, and the champagne lost by the comparison.

" In the glass of water there is no change ; it has the same properties to-day which belonged to it when God brewed it in his crucible at the dawn of creation, and flung it out in purple, cradled in vermilion, baptized in molten gold, swathed in dew, and set it as a bow of promise from sea to land. Behold it ! See its purity ! how it glitters and sparkles, as if a mass of liquid gems ! This pure, cold water, essence of life ! Brewed by our heavenly Father's hand, in the green glade, in the grassy dell, where the wild deer wander, and the lambkins play.

"Down,down in the deepest valleys,where the fountains murmur, and the rills sing, and high up the tall mountain tops, where the naked granite glitters like silver in the sunlight. Where the storm clouds brood, and the thunders crash, and away far out in the sea, where the hurricanes howl music, and the waves war in chorus, heralding the march of God. Eight of oxygen to one of hydrogen by weight, and one of oxygen to two of hydrogen by volume, cried God as he touched the mountain with his omnipotent finger, and the Amazon and Mississippi rolled their mighty floods, and pearly pebbles and dreary wastes, in obedience to the divine behests.

"There is not a cataract that flings its white foam from mountain crest to the rivulet whispering through the bed of violets, but sings this eternal law.

"There is not a wild wave lashing itself into sparkling spray against the rocky cleft, to the murmuring brooklet in which the child plays with its naked feet, but swells the measured music of the Omnipotent command. Always the same. Freeze it into ice as hard as the granite of the eternal hills, dissipate it into vapor of such exquisite tenuity, that it would take a thousand acres of the floating mist, to form a single drop of dew ; take from the high billows of the sounding sea, or from the salt solitudes of the distant ocean, bring it from the dark depths of the dreary Libyan desert, or with Guy Lusac in yon balloon, bottled up forty thousand feet above the earth's surface, still the same. Its properties never vary. Pure and sparkling as when it trembled on the lily's leaf, or faded from the snow wreath, in the golden light of the rising sun.

"Or weaving the many-colored iris, that seraph's zone of the sky, whose warp is the rain-drop of the earth, whose woof is the sunbeam of heaven, all decorated with celestial flowers, by the mystic hand of refraction. Still unchanged, ever beautiful, and the friend of man ; cooling his fevered brow, quenching his burning thirst. Lifegiving water ! No poison bubbles on its brim, no drunkard's shrieking ghost curses it in words of despair.

"Beautiful, pure, blessed, and glorious, the same sparkling, life-giving, cold water."

Many who have listened to Uniac, have asked whether this tribute was original, and given on the spot without preparation. We have reason to believe that he expected to attend this supper, and knowing he would be called on for a speech, prepared himself for the occasion. He undoubtedly gave a tribute to cold water, but probably different from the one above. A soldier who was present at the supper, says he well remembers Uniac gave a tribute to cold water, of a most eloquent character, but cannot tell whether it was the same as he heard him give afterwards throughout the country.

There has been much discussion among the temperance public, in regard to a tribute to cold water, given many years before Uniac was heard of.

A clergyman of the Methodist denomination, who travelled through the Western States, in the early days of the temperance reform, by the name of Paul Denton, is said to have advertised a grand barbecue to take place in a certain grove. He issued his invitations far and wide, and at the bottom of the bill he published, were these words, "And to all who attend, the best drink in the world will be furnished, free." A large crowd gathered, and soon the men who came for the drink, cried out,

"Your Reverence has lied; where is the drink?" Near
the grove was a spring of pure cold water, and when the
cry became loud, and promised to break up the meeting,
Mr. Denton arose, and pointing his long finger to the
spring, said : —

"There is the drink I promised, not in simmering stills,
over smoky fires, choked with poisonous gases, and surrounded with the stench of sickening odors and rank
corruptions, doth your Father in heaven prepare the
precious essence of life, the pure cold water, but in the
green glade and grassy dell, where the red deer wanders,
and the child loves to play, there God brews it; and
down, low down in the deep valleys where the fountains
murmur and the rills sing; and high up on the tall mountain-tops, where the naked granite glitters like gold in
the sun, where the storm-cloud broods and the thunder-
storms crash; and away far out on the wide, wild sea,
where the hurricane howls music, and the big waves roar
the chorus, sweeping the march of God, — there he brews
it, that beverage of life, health-giving water. And everywhere it is a thing of beauty; gleaming in the dew-drop;
singing in the summer rain; shining in the ice-gem, till
the trees all seem turned to living jewels, — spreading a
golden veil over the setting sun, or a white gauze around
the midnight moon; sporting in the cataract; sleeping in
the glacier; dancing in the hail shower; folding its
bright snow-curtains softly about the wintry world; and
weaving the many-colored iris, that seraph's zone of the
sky, whose warp is the rain-drop of earth, whose roof is
the sunbeam of heaven, all decked with celestial flowers,

by the mystic hand of refraction. Still always it is beautiful — that blessed life-water! No poison bubbles on its brink; its foam brings not madness and murder; no blood stains its liquid glass; pale widows and starving orphans weep not burning tears in its depths; no drunkard's shrieking ghost from the grave curses it in words of eternal despair! Speak out, my friends! would you exchange it for the demon's drink, Alcohol?"

We have no means of knowing whether the above story is true or not, but we find it published in a temperance Speaker, and as it **may** throw some light on the subject, we have given it.

We now find in an account **of** a meeting held at Tremont Temple, many years ago, the following, published in the papers of that day.

Mr. John B. Gough spoke on temperance last evening, at Tremont Temple, and near the close of his eloquent address he stepped to the table and taking up a glass of cold water, gave the following thrilling and eloquent tribute to cold water.

"Look at it, ye thirsty ones **of earth**, see its purity! How it glistens as if a mass of liquid gems; it is a beverage brewed by the Almighty himself. Not in the simmering still, over smoky fires, choked with poisonous gases, and surrounded by the stench of sickening odors and rank corruptions, doth your Father in heaven prepare the precious essence of life, — the pure cold water; but in the green glade and grassy dell, where the red deer wanders and the child loves to play, — there

God brews it; and down, down, in the deepest valleys, where the fountains murmur and the rills sing; and high up the tall mountain-tops where the naked granite glitters like gold in the sun, where the storm-clouds brood, and the thunder-storms crash; and away far out on the wide sea, where the hurricanes howl music, and the waves roar the chorus, sweeping the march of God, — there he brews it, that beverage of life, — health-giving water! And everywhere it is a thing of beauty; gleaming in the dew-drop; singing in the summer rain; shining in the ice-gem, till the trees all seem turned into living jewels; spreading a golden veil over the setting sun, or a white gauze over the midnight moon; sporting in the cataracts; sleeping in the glaciers; dancing in the hail-shower; folding its bright snow-curtains softly about the wintry world; and weaving the many-colored iris, that seraph's zone of the sky, whose warp is the rain-drop of earth, whose woof is the sun-beam of heaven, all checkered over with celestial flowers by the mystic hand of refraction, — still always it is beautiful, that blessed life-water! No poison bubbles on the brink; its form brings no sadness or murder; no blood stains its limpid glass; broken-hearted wives, pale widows, and starving orphans, shed no tears in its depths; no drunkard's shrieking ghost from the grave curses it in the words of eternal despair; — beautiful, pure, blessed, and glorious, for ever the same sparkling, pure water!"

We have no words of comment to offer as to who was the first to give the tribute to cold water, but having

presented all three it is impossible to read them and not
feel that all three sprung from one source.

But Uniac at least may have the credit for delivering
to hundreds and thousands of people in an impassioned
manner, something which is not surpassed for beauty
and power of language.

At the close of the supper, the officers and soldiers
congratulated him on the eloquence of his speech. It
was the effect of this effort that made him decide to
enter the lecture field. His great power as an orator
was in the descriptive line, and he had no superior in
this direction.

When he came out from the room where he had faced
wine and other liquors, and had stood firmly by his
manhood and pledge, he said, "I felt like kneeling down
on the steps of the hotel, and thanking God for my
victory. It was my first real and decisive triumph, and
I felt stronger than before."

He still labored in the direction of reforming others.
He seems now to be the master over his appetite, but he
has not destroyed the demon; he only sleeps, and eternal
vigilance will be the price of his virtue and manhood.

*

CHAPTER XI.

FIRST LETTER TO BOSTON — OTHER LETTERS — EXTRACTS
FROM WRITINGS.

In this chapter will be found extracts from some of
Uniac's letters and writings, and as there are many very
beautiful passages, they will be interesting to all.

The following letter was written to Mr. Walter Keith,
of Boston, then quite a young boy; and was the first
one received by any member of this family, and was
suggested by the sending to the army of a "Soldier's
Comfort Bag," which accidentally fell into the hands of
Uniac, and shows us how much is sometimes accomplished by the smallest act, — for under God this kind
deed done by one who was not old enough to go on to
the field of battle, and do service for his country, but
who desired to do something, led to a friendship between this soldier and the family of the boy, which gave
him a home and friends when he had none elsewhere.

"CAMP DISTRIBUTION, VIRGINIA, June 11, 1864.

"WALTER L. KEITH: — Your little bag has done good
service. It has furnished a poor Union soldier with
little necessaries that are very indispensable when one
is so far from home. You say that you are not "a very
handsome boy." Now I will tell you how to be the

handsomest boy in all Boston, and the boy that will be
loved the most; but you must do just as I tell you **if**
you want to be this handsome boy. `First, love the
Lord our God with all your heart, and all your soul
and strength. Second, love all the world next to God.
Believe in the Lord Jesus Christ, and serve him without ceasing.

" When you meet boys who are in the habit of swear-
ing or doing any other naughty thing, leave them, and
ask Jesus to bless you, and lead you away from those
bad boys, and He will do it. He will plant flowers in
your path. He will make your breath sweet, your eyes
as bright and pure as midnight stars. And he will put
so much love and sweetness in your face, that you will
be just as handsome as you will be good.

"You must love your country also, and be willing to
give your life at any moment, to defend its Constitution, to maintain its honor. Remember the great, good
men who once made a teapot of Boston harbor. They
fought hard for liberty. They won it too. Let us
maintain it.

"My time will soon be up; I was out at the first battle of Bull Run, but not as a soldier; but I joined the
army soon after, and I have seen a good deal of hard-
ship, I assure you.

"I spent four months in the **city of** Richmond; I was
there this time, twelve months ago, and celebrated the
Fourth of July there. You are a Congregationalist.
Have you ever heard of the Rev. Edward Hawes, of
Waterville, Me.? I am very fond of him. I know Mr.
—— of Boston, also; **he** is a lovely man. I would like

to write you a long letter, but I have very little time
to spare just now, so you will excuse me. I was badly
wounded at the battle of Chancellorville, twelve months
since, and I am not altogether well yet. Please send
me your picture, I will send you mine in return. You
will be my little boy, will you not? We will be fond
of each other, and when I get out of the service I
will go to Boston, and you may be certain that I will
visit you. Now I thank you for your sweet letter.
I will want you some day to send me a book if you
have it. I will tell you the name when next I write
to you.

"God bless you, and make you his especial, tender
care, and keep you from all sin, and if it be his good
pleasure, may he permit me the sweet pleasure of meeting you before long."

This beautiful letter called out an answer, to which
Uniac wrote the following letter : —

"MY DEAR YOUNG FRIEND, — God has been very
good to me of late, in surrounding me with sweet spirit-
ual influence; in breathing his peace through my heart;
in making my path more sunny, my playground broader,
and my playmates better. Walter, to be pure is to be
heavenly; and to love Jesus with our whole hearts, and
one another with tender affection, should be our end and
aim in life. You wish to know my past history. It is
full of stirring incident, but you are not yet prepared to
know it. When we meet, you will entertain me with
your favorite airs. I will entertain you with a narrative

of my life. I have much to interest you, some instructions to give you, and a good deal to tell you that will
make you sad. Do you know that it is good for us to
be sad by times? It mellows our nature. It sweetens
our disposition. It brings us closer to the cross. And
the reason why it has this influence, is because when sad
and melancholy, we seek in vain for a remedy among our
friends.

"The world has no consolation for the sorrowing heart.
Earthly hope may weave her dreamy garlands, and fringe
the future with flowers and sunshine, but all these are
perishable, the heart grows sick and sicker, until at last
it finds consolation, where alone consolation is to be
found, in the sweet teachings of our loving and gentle
Saviour. Yes, W., to be sad by times is a goodly thing.

"I am very fond of music. It has a refining influence.
It is a part of the pleasures of angels. It is the breathing of heaven. You love to go out, and sport and play.
So did I when I was young. But I hope you select good
playmates. To go with boys who swear and smoke and
chew, who are rude in their language, and ruder in their
behavior, is not good for a good boy like you. Our
future life owes much to our youthful training and prac-
tices. Would you like to have a handsome foot when
you grow up to be a man? If you would, you must not
(now, when it is soft and tender) force it into an ugly,
unnatural shoe. Should you do so, you will retard its
growth in proper proportions, and it will take the shape
of the ill-made shoe.

"Now, it is just so with your character. It sets its
shape and direction from the circumstances by which it

is surrounded. If these are good, your **character will be** meek, sweet, and Christlike. If otherwise, your character will be rough, angular, and ungodly. And the good people will not love you. Bad boys may laugh at you because you don't swear and smoke as they do, but you must remember that God does not love bad boys. And what need you care for the ill-will of those who are not loved by God?

" You should never forget your Sabbath school, and **the** good lessons that are taught there. You may get tired sometimes, and wish you were away from it. When you feel this way, just think of the story of Christ's suffering for you.

" How tenderly your father and mother love you, and how dearly you love them in return. Christ's love for you is stronger still. Won't you sit down and talk with him one hour each Sabbath? I know you will, because I feel that you are good, and this feeling makes me love you very dearly. And I know, too, that you will not associate with boys who are unwilling to love their Redeemer; should you do so, the soldiers would not love you."

The following was written to a sister of the above, and explains itself.

" I like your picture dearly, because I believe it is the picture of a good, obedient girl, and one who loves Jesus with her whole heart and soul. Am I not right in this? I know I am, and I shall therefore love you the more tenderly.

7

"Is n't God very good to us? **What** a magnificent world he has spread out before us, with what a rich carpet he has covered it for the summer months, and what lots of *bouquets* he has scattered here and there, and how kindly he waters them with crystal dew while they slumber. What grand hues and tints He breathes through them as they float in the breeze, and fill the air with unapproachable fragrance.

"And how He changes the looks of everything in autumn, to resemble *molten gold*. This lasts for its season, and pleases the eye, — when behold the entire face of Nature is clothed in spotless white. O, how grateful we should feel towards the Being who is thus kind to us. And you must remember also that He painted your lips with inimitable vermilion, and gave a rosy roundness to your eye, which no artist can imitate in beauty and color.

"You love this God, don't you? and you love and heed your mother and your father, and your good dear brother, and you pray for all of them, don't you?

"This is the way to be a good girl, to be loved and admired by every good person. You will have no occasion to have anything to say or do with unchristian people, except to advise them of their folly.

"I have been growing worse for the last week, instead of better, but I am in hopes that I will be well soon. I anticipate much pleasure from your company when I go to Boston. We will have some pleasant walks together, will we not?

"I want to see Cambridge, and Bunker Hill, and Mount Auburn Cemetery, and a great many other places, so that you must be prepared to spend some time in my company. I received a letter yesterday from A. F. ——— Esq. I have written to him to come and see me by all means. Will you give my love to Walter, and to your good mother, and to all your family?

"And will you excuse your sick soldier's poor letter? I think of you very often. You will think of me by times, and believe me, that my prayers will be constantly offered in your behalf, that Jesus may be near you at all times, that the angels of love and peace may take you in their ward and keeping. That your life may be long and happy, and that your crown may be a garland of never-dying light and verdure. Can I wish you any more? If I can, 't is wished.

"Accept my love, and believe me to be, your ever affectionate friend."

The following are extracts from letters to a friend residing at Boston, and were written soon after signing the pledge. And though they may repeat a few facts we have stated, nevertheless they will repay a perusal.

"CONVALESCENT CAMP, near Alexandria.

"Jan. 21st, 1864. Thus far in life has mine been a career of madness, of dreadful dissipation; nor have I yet been subjected to any ordeal that would test the sincerity of my reformation.

"I am to speak in the city of Alexandria next week; the occasion will be a presentation and social supper. It will afford me an opportunity of testing my power of resisting ' mine ancient foe.'

" If I be the victor, I will look the future in the face, firm in faith.

"Jan. 29th. I spoke at the Marshall House in Alexandria, afterwards I sat down to a social supper. I was the only temperate man present, and am glad to tell you that I had no desire to indulge, though pressed to do so.

" We had a large party and some very distinguished men.

"Jan. 29. I was taken prisoner at the three days' fight at Chancellorsville, by the 43d Georgia. I was wounded on the first day, and twice on the third. I was reported killed in the Adjutant's report. I was entirely helpless, being both wounded and paralyzed.

" My friends left me for dead, and my foes began to search after my effects.

" In so doing they discovered a Masonic emblem on my person, when the Lieutenant in command desired them to desist.

"He made a personal examination, after which he had me removed to a place of safety. I was conscious of all that was transpiring, but could neither move nor yet articulate a single sound.

" I spent the most part of three months in the prison of Richmond. Before I went there I weighed one hundred and thirty-eight pounds, when I came to Annapolis I only weighed seventy-eight pounds. What I suffered cannot be told. We all lived in the shadow of starvation.

" Apr. 28th. I enclose a temperance pledge. Keep it in memory of me. I signed a similar one. Pray God that I may keep it.

" May 6th. Twelve months ago to-day, and I was on my way to Richmond. I pant to be with my command once more. I asked for an examination in the hope that I would be sent forward, but I did not succeed except in obtaining the pleasant information 'that I had the heart disease.'

" Be prepared to hear startling war news in a few days. **Lee** is far seeing, and perfectly at home in Virginia.

" Grant will have to exercise immense caution, or he gets flanked on the Rapidan.

" May 20th. The scenery all around here is delightful, that is to one who has the soul to feel it, the heart to beat with it, the ears to hear it, the eyes to see **its** many shades and hues.

" This is a charming vale resembling Avoca, my usual evening ramble. How rich in verdure, fragrant with magnolias, and musical with the song of birds and insects !

" Yonder mountain has flung this stream from her stony lap, freighted with water-lilies, and sent it bounding and sparkling through the rich plain.

" It is called ' Four Mile Run.' Descending this hill of green, one obtains a nearer view of the Potomac. There it lies below us, smooth, broad, and yellow, more formidable as a defence to the Capitol, than would be a million warriors armed, equipped and ' eager for the fray.' To the right is the city of Alexandria, with its uninviting mien. And to the left, Washington. There stands

the Capitol, like a bright eye in the forehead of a brazen
monster, and nearer to the Potomac and farther to the
left is the unfinished 'Stony Finger,' intended to per-
petuate the memory of Nature's noblest man.

"The sun is just setting. It hangs like a globe of
molten gold from the brow of the far off west."

The following poem was written by Mr. U., after one
of his visits to the Soldiers' Cemetery, Arlington,
Va. : —

THE MEMORY OF THE BURIED BRAVE.

The memory of the buried brave,
  O, shrine it in your soul forever;
The hero of an honored grave,
  Is like the rock wrapped in the river,
Spreading o'er Time's e'er fleeting wave,
  The spirit of his life forever.
'Gainst brutal force and crafty scheme,
  An everlasting war he wages,
And like the foam-fleet on the stream,
  Each glowing hope, each brilliant dream,
  Flows down to future ages.

At length, the stately millions learn
  The moral of their own dark story,
That, while the servile court the stern,
  And lose, for gold, their love for glory,
New chains are all such slaves can earn,
  Save cruel death, and burial gory.
But when the brave, the bold, the good,
  Are banded in true patriot labor,
They feel the iron in their blood.
  O, each who died for nation-hood,
  Was gathered strangely from the flood,
  To form a conquering sabre.

To conquer mind, to chain the will,
  Shall be without one sane believer,
A creed that mocks fixed nature, still
  Is but a base and false deceiver.
Truth shall bend no suppliant knee
  To wrong and riot; they must falter!
The very ashes of the free
  Give rapid growth to liberty.
What marvel happier days shall see,
  Each nameless grave an altar.

O 'er ruined hopes let tyrants laugh,
  And quaff their wine o'er baffled merit.
The strong winds humbled by the chaff,
  Is ay the dream that fools inherit,
They cannot steal the epitaph
  Graved on the marble of man's spirit.
There it abides the promised hour,
  When earth shall be aroused and bidden
Of Heaven, to hurl down tyrant power.
  From freedom's meadow, mead, and bower,
  Slavery's home and lordly tower,
  It shall by God be driven.

The memory of the buried brave,
  The last fond twilight streak adorning,
The hero of an honored grave,
  Is first to send around the warning.
Freedom by the South long deemed dead,
  Is bursting forth in orient morning.
O'er that memory shrined in tears,
  Which few save God regard with sadness,
The dew no mortal sees nor hears,
Until the rosy morn appears,
Is still the loveliest thing that wears
  The light of morning gladness.

Then follows a letter from a Western paper, **written**
to a lady, and published by her, which we **have taken
the** liberty to insert.

"CAMP DISTRIBUTION, VA., Aug. 5, **1864.**

"*Miss* —— ——, *Weston, Wood County, Ohio.*

"DEAR MISS,— I am a soldier, and an entire stranger to you, and even to your place of residence. Not only is this true, but we may ever remain so, and yet I am tempted to write to you, and I feel assured that in so doing, you will not be offended at my imprudence. I have been a wanderer from my very childhood, and have spent much of my time amid the wild scenes of nature, where by close observation I have endeavored to hold close communion with God. Solitary dells have been the altars whereat I have worshipped, and the deeper feelings of my nature have borrowed a hue from their sweet loneliness.

"Nor have the wild storms of the three years' campaign through which I have passed, and in which, I assure you, I have suffered, been able to crush out my love of romance. Each day but makes the sheen of the grass greener, the emerald of the dew purer and brighter; and each hour of my life is gilded with a holier and a softer tinge.

"During my walks yesterday, I came across a lonely graveyard. I entered — there were three graves. Two of them contained the ashes of Robert and Emma Frazer, as the little stones at the head indicated. The third was the grave of their mother, and the monument bore the following inscription: "To the memory of Presha Lee Frazer, consort of Anthony R. Frazer. Born Dec. 25th, 1799. Died Sep. 26th, 1859.

"I examined the white monument. **It bore a snowy**

wreath, and right over the wreath in pencil mark, was written the name, 'Miss —— ——, Weston, Wood County, Ohio, and underneath it, and close to the wreath, the name of " Miss —— ——' of the same place.

"Both names were written by the same hand. I began to reflect, — these names were written by a soldier. What has become of the hand that penned them? Has it been stilled forever, or does it still grasp the musket, and is it ready to do its duty? Whatever be its fate, I will write to those parties, and let them know that some soldier has been remembering them, while loitering around this lone 'city of the dead.'

"I found the name of 'Hiram B. Smith' on another corner of the monument. **He** belonged to the Ohio troops.

"If you see Miss ——, tell her that she has been remembered, and if you wish to hear from him who has made so free as to write you this, you or she may do so at any time by directing a note to 'E. H. Uniac, Camp Distribution, Va., care of Christian Commission.'"

To this letter he received an answer, full of gratitude, and also informed him how much good his letter had done; for, says the writer, "It has inspired the women of our town **to** form a society to aid and work for the soldiers."

He seemed to long for sympathy, and the tendrils of his nature ran out in every direction for it. At the close of a day when he had been having an unusually hard fight, he wrote the following words in his diary. "I have been wandering to-day, over the green fields and by

the murmuring brooks; I have plucked the sweetest
flowers, I have gazed on the blue ethereal vault of
heaven, — and on everything, from the modest violet to
the hilly range of clouds in the sky, I read passing away.
Yes, men go and men come, to-day we are and to-morrow we are not, and yet God has strewn all around us
much that is beautiful, to inspire us to noble action.
And when I have had such a day of desperate struggling
as I have had to-day, I think of the worn and weary that
have passed through the struggles of this world, and to-
night are resting under the shade of the 'Tree of Life,'
and I confess I sometimes long to be there. I feel I
would rather die now, when I am sober and in my right
mind, than to go back to what I have suffered; and still,
in the face of all my bitter experience, I often fear I shall
be conquered in the fight. God forbid! is my hourly,
yes, my constant prayer. The following beautiful lines
have been running in my mind to-day.

> " Where the faded flower shall blossom,
>   Blossom never more to fade,
> Where the shaded sun shall brighten,
>   Brighten, never more to shade," —

there our struggles, trials, and heartaches shall be over,
and **we** shall sit and sing, and 'go no more out forever.' "

CHAPTER XII.

HIS FIRST VISIT TO MASSACHUSETTS — SPEECH, ETC.

In the summer of 1865, Mr. Uniac came to Boston for the first time. It was brought about through a correspondence which had been begun through the sending of what was called a comfort-bag by a son of Mr. Martin L. Keith, of Boston, to which we have alluded. Extracts of that correspondence are to be found in another part of the book, and show the deep friendship that had sprung up between him and the family, and his coming was anxiously looked for; and when on the 17th of June, with carpet-bag in hand, he made his appearance, he was cordially welcomed to this pleasant and comfortable home. He was well cared for, assisted to some articles of apparel which he very much needed, and everything done to make him contented and comfortable.

The family became so attached to him, that Mr. and Mrs. Keith offered him a home with them as long as he remained in this vicinity.

July 4, 1865, he made his first speech in Massachusetts, at Abington, which was well received, and he received calls from all parts of Plymouth County. He left the house of Mr. Keith July 9th, to visit a prominent gentleman of Boston; not returning that night, the family began to feel anxious for him, for the struggle

with his appetite was fearful at this time. He did **not**
return for nearly a week, when he came back, sick, sor-
rowful, and discouraged. The enemy had conquered
him, and this was his first fall since he signed the
pledge.

His dear friends that he had made received him kindly,
and treated him tenderly, and while weeping like a child,
he solemnly and faithfully promised never to yield again
to the intoxicating cup. He was taken to the Washing-
tonian Home, where he remained and grew stronger and
better. From here he went to New Hampshire, and
spent the season ; then came back and went to lecturing
in good earnest for temperance. September 3 he spoke
at Swampscott, October 8 at the Park Street Sunday
school, Boston, October 15 at Lawrence, and in all parts
of New England and the West, and was everywhere well
spoken of by the press.

"Zion's Herald" of July, 1865, said, "Mr. Uniac has the
fire, feeling, and native eloquence of his nation ; experience and observation in the army, and the abundant grace
of God' being superadded, leaves little to be desired."

Chicago paper says : "Bro. Uniac of Boston made one
of the best addresses. The audience were charmed by
his eloquence." He was now speaking in the West, having left Massachusetts October 16, 1865, and his success
throughout the great West was unparalleled.

He went almost entirely unheralded, a perfect stranger,
and spoke on a subject which requires a master exponent
to interest the general public.

The Indianapolis "Gazette" and "Journal," and in fact
all the papers west, spoke of him in the highest terms, and

we will not take **space and time** by referring to **them** further.

On the 8th of December he arrived back in Boston, made his first speech to a Boston audience, in Tremont Temple, on the evening of December 19, 1865, of which speech the Boston " Daily Advertiser " said, " His remarks were of a very interesting nature, and at times of a feeling and fervent description." The " Boston Post " said, " For upwards of an hour he held the closest attention of the audience while he portrayed with a startling vividness, the evils of indulgence in intoxicating drinks. The " Journal " of a later date, speaking of his lecture before the Young Men's Christian Association, said, in concluding its report of his speech, " Mr. Uniac spoke somewhat over an hour in a most eloquent **strain.**"

In fact the press and the public were unanimous in the conclusion that he was destined to stand at the head of descriptive orators in the country, provided he **was** able to overcome his desire for strong drink.

While he was speaking one night at South Reading, a very touching incident occurred, and as it well illustrates the power he sometimes had over very hardened men, we will relate it. After he had closed his lecture, a young man came upon the platform and taking his hand, said : —

"It is a strange thing that I am here. I have kept the vilest place and sold the most rum of any man in this town.

"I have led young men and old men to destruction. A few weeks ago, I cursed every man who spoke against my business. I defied God. But soon after I could not sleep. The thought haunted me that some of the men I

had made drunk at night might be dead at my door in
the morning. But thank God I **am** converted." He
then raised both his hands and said, **"I** promise before
God Almighty, my Maker and Saviour, that I will never
sell or use another single drop of liquor while God gives
me life."

He went on to say that he was born near there; that
he had been a soldier and wounded, and had a little
family. "You have a right," he said, "to hate them and
me; I know you do hate us; but for God's sake won't
you love us for the future? I had a good Christian
mother."

Here he broke down, and the eloquent Irish orator
happily took up the thread of discourse and carried still
higher the tide of feeling in the assembly by alluding to
the tear of penitence brought by the angel in Tom
Moore's "Peri Pardoned," as a passport of re-entrance at
the gate of Paradise.

It was said by one who was present that this was one
of the most thrilling speeches he ever listened to.

One other incident of a similar nature occurred one
night, when, after he had retired to his hotel from a public
meeting, and had seated himself in front of the fire, some
one rapped on his door; he opened it, and found a lady
there closely véiled; she said, "Your speech has had such
an effect on my husband that he desires to see you at our
house." He put on his coat and followed her, and found
her husband to be a notorious rumseller, who had made
up his mind under the influence of Mr. Uniac's speech to
quit the business and to sign the pledge, and said he
wanted to do it in the presence of Mr. Uniac; and there

in the presence of his two children he vowed **to** be a better man, and to this day, from anything we know to the contrary, has kept his pledge ; and upon no heart did the news of Mr. Uniac's fall and death come with a more crushing weight than on this man.

These incidents, and hundreds of others that might be added, prove that he was showing fruits of his labors. He was now fairly in the work, speaking every night and laboring incessantly ; and yet, in the midst of all this, is it not strange that his appetite often raged with almost uncontrollable power ?

Invitations now came to **him** from all parts of **the** country, and he had to refuse many for lack of time to accept them. He had everywhere made a good impression.

The following is an extract from **one of his first** lectures in Massachusetts : —

"God works in his own wondrous way. Beneath the sea His hand is visible, and islands are flung to the sunlight, by the might of that hand. The geography of the globe is changing. The veil of the human mind is rent. Planets that were fixed in the constellations at Creation's dawn, have been visible for the **first** time in the history of man.

"The human soul has broader pinions, the human perceptions greater depths, the human imagination soars to a purer, sublimer height, than it ever soared before. Eighteen hundred years of Christian civilization has done something for humanity. Before Christ came, genius leaped and quivered in a thousand brilliant corus-

cations, but went **out** into a night of eternal darkness.
It was like the dew of night falling upon the arid mountain. The mountain returned no sweet verdure. The
cold winds blew, the dew was changed into ice, the bleak
rocks glistened, but the sun came and dissolved the ice ;
the rocks were naked and forbidding as ever.

" Christ came, His words fell like dew upon the wood-
land vale, the withered leaf leaped into life, and the
sleeping grapes stood erect to kiss the feet of the Master. We have seen the glory of the coming of Christian
truth. All parts of the world are being blessed by the
rays of the sun of righteousness, and still, in this land
of Bibles, the demon of intemperance is felt everywhere,
blasting and ruining the strength and glory of the land.
Let us gather inspiration and hope from God's truth, to
renew the battle for crushed and bleeding humanity.
Lift up the fallen, help the weak, and souls redeemed
will sing in heaven, as the fruits of our labor."

The following story brings us to the consideration of
an important question in the life of Uniac.

During the war, all those who loved our flag and
country were anxious to do something to aid the
cause of liberty and union ; even the smallest children
were busy holding fairs, and in various ways collecting
money for the comfort of the soldiers. Two little children, six years of age, residing in North Brookfield,
Mass., collected money enough to buy a Bible to send to
the soldiers. It was a very neat, well-bound book. On
the fly-leaf was written something like this : " Should this
be instrumental, under God, in the conversion of the sol-

dier into whose hands it may fall, will he please write ..
letter to us ; " to which was signed the names of the children.

It was placed in a box with other articles, and fell into
the hands of Uniac. He carried it with him everywhere
he went, and by the light of the camp-fires at night, was
often seen poring over its pages.

He read it as he never read the Bible before. He
resolved to change his life, and he believed that it was
this little gift from the hands of these dear children,
that led to his conversion. So he resolved to write the
children a letter, which he did, full of tenderness and
thankfulness ; and from this there began a correspondence
with the family, which ended in a dear friendship. The
Rev. Mr. Keene, now of Franklin, Mass., was the pastor
of these children, and has often spoken of how much good
was done by this little act. This Bible is in existence
in this State, and is highly prized by those who have it.
This little story enforces the lesson, that none are too
young to do something to aid and benefit mankind.

The relating of the above brings us to a subject
which cannot be avoided in writing a true story of
Uniac's life, and that is, his religious belief, and his
standing in regard to the same. We do not feel quali-
fied to stand in any light as a judge over a man's conscience, or religious belief, but as it was understood at
one time, that Mr. Uniac had professed to be a changed
and converted man, and that he had fallen away from
the same, we desire to give his true condition, as we
understand it.

His sorrow for his sins was deep and heartfelt. We

8

have heard him **pour out** his soul in prayer and agony, when he thought of the disgrace that his course might bring on the church of Christ. He felt that he was unworthy, and often expressed it, but still he clung to the hope that had found a place in his heart, and though sometimes almost gone, it is doubtful if it was ever entirely extinguished.

One clergyman has said since his death, " Don't you know that the Bible says, ' No drunkard shall enter the kingdom of Heaven?'" In reply we have to say, that for four months previous 'to his death, he was a sober, upright man, engaged in a war to keep himself from being a drunkard, and it can therefore be said, that there **was** something sublime in the contest, and while none felt more keenly the utter sinfulness of much that he had done, we are content to leave him in the hands of Him who took upon himself the form of man, and who knows all our weaknesses and frailties. "Judge not, that ye be not judged." Is there no reward for struggles with sin that are unsuccessful? Is a soldier's grave less sacred and dear because he fell when our flag went down, **and** defeat came to our arms? Was not his heroism grander, and his courage put to a severer test, to fight against great odds, especially when he had been overcome many times by the same enemy? We are too apt to make success a criterion by which to judge the efforts of a man.

Who does not know that the noblest men are **those** who have been overcome? When the history **of our** lives shall be read in the clear light of heaven, we **shall** doubtless find that easy victories **are** of less **real worth,** than hard and desperate fought battles where we have gone down in the struggle, and triumph has seemed to be with our enemy.

It was not his habit to write out in full his speeches, therefore some of his most brilliant passages lived only in his memory, and died with him.

We have, however, been able to procure several, that were reported *verbatim* for the press, and give a good idea of his power and eloquence.

The following address was delivered at Lynn, Mass., one Sabbath evening, shortly before he fell, but of course many of his finest illustrations and most powerful passages are lost. But it partakes of his genius, and is therefore interesting : —

"LADIES AND GENTLEMEN, — 'Men die, and principles live.' When you and I have passed away, the principles we helped to forward, if they are formed in right, will live on.

"Immortality is written on every good deed and word; and when the earth is no more, when the stars have lost their brightness, and the sun ceases to shine, truth will stand, and not be moved. I appear before you to-night to say something to aid the cause of temperance. I am deeply interested in this subject. I have felt and seen the evils of intemperance as few men have. I am not old, and yet God only knows to what depths of misery and sin I have sunken ; and as I stand here to-night, and think of the pit from whence I have been digged, and see around me so many who are ready to help and sustain me, I am constrained to thank God for his goodness and mercy towards me.

"I have been asked to give some incidents to-night
from my own life. I am willing to tell the story of the
dark days through which I have passed, but I never
speak of them without feeling my cheeks tingle with
shame, that so much of my life has been lost, yes, worse
than lost, — squandered. I regard the years that I was
under the control of rum, as a blank in my existence,
dark and awful. I shudder when I think how deep the
iron has entered into my heart. Oh! my friends, I have
often prayed for the rocks and mountains to fall on me
and hide me, so wretched was I; and therefore, as I
revert to those days, I cannot repress a feeling of loath-
ing and almost disgust for myself and those associated
with me in the crime and degradation of my years of
intemperate drinking. Again, I repeat, I do not like to
refer to my days of dissipation and ruin, and would not,
did I not think I might thereby be instrumental in saving some young men who hear me, from going where I
have wandered, and suffering what I have suffered. I
cannot begin to express in language the feeling I have
for the men who led me on, step by step, by associating
with me while my money lasted, and the moment I
needed help, cast me off. I have stood in the streets of
New York, with nowhere to lay my aching, weary head,
homeless and friendless. I have stood thus, and seen
those men who have had the benefit of my money, when
I was using it freely and unsparingly, pass me by without so much as noticing me by a nod; and I want to tell
the flashy young men whom the bar-keeper receives with
a hearty shake of the hand, and a pleasant smile, that if
by his stock in trade you become unfortunate, you will

be kicked from his store, and not be known by him, when he meets you on the street. I know this is so, for I have felt the cutting of this kind, as few have, for my nature is sensitive to the slightest touch. What these men want is your money, and there is no use to talk of friendship formed over the wine-cup. It is not lasting nor real. I remember, one bitter cold night, I had been drinking hard all day, and this evening had spent all my money in a saloon, and when it came time for the shop to be closed, I was told by the keeper to 'travel.' I begged to sleep on the floor, anywhere; but no, I was taken, and by force shoved into the street. I wandered up and down the street for about an hour, when I saw the door of a place where horses were kept, open.

"I made the best of my way there, and crept into a corner where there was some hay or straw, and went to sleep. Early in the morning, the man who came to feed the horses, discovered me, and told me to get out. I looked up at him, and saw in a moment that he was one of my professed friends while I had money, and now that I had none he would not let me sleep with his horses. I repeat it, there is no real friendship among such men; they will shun you, after they help ruin you.

"In 1860 I found myself homeless, and a vagabond in the streets of New York; but I was not always in that condition. I stood, as many of these young men stand, thinking myself safe, while I sailed on the river of moderate drinking, without one thought of the danger below. Friends cried out for me to stop, but I heeded not their warning voices. I said, ' I will stop before it is too late,' as some of you have often said.

" Were you ever at Niagara Falls? I have stood spellbound, as I have looked at the mighty rushing and foaming of the water, as it went seething, boiling, and tumbling over the rapids and falls, sending mountains high the white spray, which by the magic hand of refraction was turned into all the colors of the rainbow, making the grandest scene mortal eye ever gazed upon.

" After I had feasted my eyes on this sight for a little, the guide asked me to walk up the bank of the river, and he would show me the place where a few years ago a sad accident happened to two lovely boys. A mother and these children were visiting this place, and the boys got into a boat to row along the bank, to collect some flowers. Unconsciously they neared the rapids, when their mother lifted up her voice, urging them to return ; but they knew when to turn, they said, and still rowed on, when all at once the boat was tossed hither and thither, and to their great surprise they found themselves in the midst of the rapids. They grasped the oars, and pulled for dear life, but too late ! too late ! They looked and saw their mother kneeling on the bank, praying for them. One more look, and over the falls they went, lost to friends and home forever.

" Let me tell you, moderate drinkers, here this evening, you are on a more dangerous river than those boys who went over the falls. It was such an impressive temperance lecture, that I never forgot it. Yes, when I began to think of my course, the fear I should die a drunkard took hold of me so powerfully that I would kneel down and ask God to help me to reform.

"**You,** who have not felt the awful feeling that comes over the poor drunkard, when he realizes the low condition he has placed himself in, and feels his power **to** lift himself up gone, cannot comprehend my condition at this time; if there is one here situated as I was then, perhaps he may appreciate my case. I do not refer to these days with any other feeling than of shame and . sadness.

"I **regret** to say, that I have seen and heard men tell their experience in such a manner as to give the impression that they were, on the whole, proud of their course. **But** God forbid I should tell this story in any other way, except with deep humiliation and sorrow.

"But, my friends, I feel to-night like letting the 'dead past bury its dead'; and, God helping me, I mean to act in the present, and try in the future to redeem the past.   .

"God forbid that I should glory amid so much shame. I have walked through villages and heard the ringing laugh of the returning school-children, and as I looked on them in all their purity, untainted by the touch of sin, and unpolluted by crime, O, how my whole soul and body prayed God to keep them from what I have passed through! for a man can never be so pure and good again, who has felt the fire on his heart. And so do I plead to-night with the young, to not enter into the shadows of this great evil; to give all their life to virtue and temperance, to keep themselves pure as the snow on the mountains nearest the clouds.

"Did you ever on a clear night stand on some hill and gaze at the stars? And as you have looked at the countless numbers of little stars that only just show their light, have you never thought that perhaps they are larger and more beautiful than the sun itself? for the most beautiful things of earth are seen the least. So let these young men who are not bright and shining lights in this age, remember God sees the little stars in all their glory and grandeur. He knows how large they are, and so every good deed you do for yourselves or your weak neighbor may not be visible to the eye of man, but God sees and rewards you. Remember, no matter where God has put us in the world, he expects us to do our whole duty, to follow out the noble promptings of the heart which tells us to go into all the world and help those who are unfortunate. Yes, ' Dare to be true, Dare to be noble, Dare to be right.'

"My friends, this cause is God's holy cause. In its behalf the most sincere prayers are going up to Heaven every day from worse than broken hearts. Yes, from crushed and bleeding hearts, from those whose sky of life is starless, around whose homes no flowers bloom, no birds sing, and happy voices of children are unknown; but they pray for you and for me, and as the wife looks on one she has loved, once noble and generous, and of whom she was proud, when she stood by his side and heard him promise to love, honor, and protect her while life should last, now sunk low in the scale of humanity, almost like the very beast, she does not cease to hope and pray for his redemption, and for the prosperity of this great work.

"There are homes for us to brighten, hearts from which to lift the burden of despair, forsaken and starving

children to look after and care for, and to save from ever
touching the accursed cup of death. And the field is
white for the harvest, and indeed it is true that the
laborers are few. All around us on every breeze comes
the cry for help. We want *men*, — self-sacrificing men, —
men of large hearts and strong hands, who are ready to
do with their might whatever their hands find to do.
Why, for a moment, suppose all those who profess
to love Christ should awake to the enormity of the great
evil of intemperance, and resolve to do all they could to
wash it out, what would be the result? We would
shake this country from centre to circumference, and in
the shaking, drive every man engaged in the rum business out of it, and the air of America would be fragrant
with the principle of total abstinence.

"Let us fling out the truth, write it in letters of living
light by day, and fire by night. Let the press bear it to
the remotest corner of civilization. Let temperance
literature be scattered as leaves of autumn. Let the
pupil thunder in its defence. Yes, let the truth be borne
aloft on the wings of every breeze. Let us catch inspiration from the glorious opportunities opening before us,
for work and for noble action. Let those who sigh for
higher horizons, and wider fields, labor where they are;
and, sir, we shall have our reward, not only in the fact
that we have done our duty, but that we have helped
some one else to come up higher in the fight, and he that
is instrumental in saving a soul it shall cover a multitude
of sins."

CHAPTER XIII.

PERSONAL EXPERIENCE — HARD STRUGGLES — SPEECHES,
EXTRACTS, ETC.

THOUGH he was now fairly in the temperance work,
and the public seemed to have the greatest confidence in
his ability to stand, his nearest friends knew that he stood
as it were upon the brink of a precipice. He would
often come to me, and taking my hand say, " O, I need
your help and sympathy, my old enemy is raging." At
times when hardly any one thought of his falling, his
intimate personal friends were often called to go with him
on some of his lecture tours, so fearful was he that if
left alone, he would not be able to withstand the temptations that were surrounding him. I well remember, one
day in 1867, while he was speaking for prohibition in
Massachusetts, he had an engagement in Worcester
County. Just before the train started, he called on me ;
his face was pale, and his eyes looked as though he had
been passing through an exhausting sickness. I asked
him what the matter was, and he told me in these words :
"I have been fighting ; yes, I have had almost to lock
myself into my room, and have run from my home to you,
fearing to go slowly." I took his hand, and it was covered with a cold sweat, and I saw where, in his nervous
excitement, he had drove the nails of his fingers into the

palm of his hand in his effort to conquer his appetite. He continued, "Unless you go with me to-night, I shall fall." I went, and at the conclusion of his speech he said, "I have once more come off the victor."

Knowing these facts, his ultimate fall was not a great surprise to those who knew him best. He was now considered the best temperance speaker before the public who was continually in the work.

At the battle of Antietam, Uniac was present and took part in that terrible fight, and as there were one or two very thrilling incidents which came under his observation, and which he has related to the edification of thousands all over the land, we deem it best to give the principal one in his own language, as near as possible.

At the close of a Christian convention held at Music Hall, Boston, he was called to the platform to speak, and had proceeded a few moments, when a request was placed before him, that he would give to the audience his celebrated charge at the battle of Antietam; after a few preliminary remarks, he spoke as follows : —

"Word was given to the regiment to prepare for the charge; every man stripped himself to the waist, — it was to be a desperate affair, and everything that impeded their progress must be cast aside, — knapsacks, haversacks, and blankets were flung to the ground, and the long line of beating hearts and strong arms stood with their bayonets glistening in the sun, waiting the word. It was to decide the fate of the day, perhaps the fate of the nation. It was a desperate effort of General Lee to

march through the North.   In a moment, a faint sound
could be heard, as of a distant voice ; it grew louder, and
was caught by the aids, until it reached the colonel of
the regiment, who, striking the spurs into his horse,
leaped to the front, and waving his sword, cried ' Follow
me ! forward at double quick ! ' Like lightning they
dash over the field in the face of belching cannon, while
a perfect shower of bullets rained upon their devoted
heads, thinning their ranks at every step ; still they close
up ; the first battery is reached, to take it is but the work
of a moment ; the rebel gunners are killed and scattered
in an instant, for these men are terribly in earnest, as
the blood of their comrades is flowing all around them.
There is yet a plain to cross, and one more battery to
silence ; forward they rush, over the dead and dying, —
shot and shell, canister and grape, are mowing them
down fearfully.   They do not falter nor turn ; the plain
is crossed, the battery reached, which the rebels defend
manfully, until both flags mingle in the conflict.   Now
one is up, and now the other ; at last the stars and
stripes stay up, while the stars and bars trail in the dust.
The rebel line begins to falter, stagger from right to left ;
the centre breaks ; the enemy is flying ; the day is ours ;
the country honored, and the little band of the regiment
who have survived the charge, rest on their arms on
the dearly bought ground, wet with precious blood,
while the sun has gone down, and the stars of heaven
are looking pityingly down on the dying and the
dead."

It is the night after the battle, and those who are spared
and have kind hearts go over the field to minister unto

those who are suffering distress and agony, and among those thus nobly engaged, is Uniac; and as he wanders over this terrible spot, the weak voice of a dying man calling to him, attracts his attention; he hastens to his side, and resting his head on his lap, listens to his story. 'I have fought my last fight, knowing that I shall not see those I love again. Comrade, take a message to these dear friends of mine.' By a desperate effort he raises himself, takes a locket which is concealed under his coat, and straining his eyes, now almost glassy with the touch of death, he kisses it, hands it to Uniac, and says 'Take this to my mother,' and, as a smile of triumph sparkled in his eye, said 'Tell her to thank God I was not conquered by intemperance, but shall fill an honored soldier's grave'; and his spirit had gone to the camping grounds of heaven. This scene so affected him, that he said, as he learned more of the dead soldier's life, that it was one of the best temperance lectures he ever heard. It must have been a help, struggling as he was with his life's enemy, for here was a man praising God, even in death, that he had escaped the drunkard's awful fate. There were other thrilling incidents connected with this bloody field through which he passed, and he said in after years, that in the midst of all these exciting times, there was one thought ringing in his ears, which was, 'Shall I escape all these perils and at last be conquered by rum?' Who shall say that he did not struggle and labor for his own salvation? Earth's grandest heroes are found amid the struggling, weak, and weary-hearted men who are trying to conquer themselves. In referring to himself one evening, he said : —

" In, 1861, I joined the army, but its fortunes did not make me a sober man; on the contrary, I revelled in crime, being sober only when intoxicating liquors were kept from me by army regulations. By the mercy of God, in the thirteen battles in which I was engaged, I was a sober man; in the last of these battles I was taken prisoner, and was obliged for six months to share the horrors of Libby Prison and Belle Island.

"While in this desolate condition, the example of a comrade, who had gone forth under the same flag, and had braved the same dangers with me, made a deep impression on my mind. He was shot by the rebel guard for taking a piece of food, just as he was about to put it to his lips. It was a terrible sight. His dying words were, 'I have kept the pledge, and die in the faith of my Maker.'

"Every day of my life I made resolutions to reform, and abandon drinking, but they were soon broken. But when I abandoned my own strength, and fell on my knees before Christ, and trusted upon divine aid alone, then was I enabled to break loose from temptation, and become a sober man."

In 1867 and 1868, he spoke in various parts of the country, quite often appearing before lyceums. The following is an extract from a speech on the temperance question delivered at Tremont Temple not very long before his fall.

" This is a period in the history of the country when all men should feel sober; this is eminently a time for persons to think and act with sobriety in all things. We should not rely too much on the enthusiasm of **the mo-**ment, emanating from high sources in the country.

"Besides this, it is the duty of temperance men to give facts to the people. The question naturally arises, both to the speaker and the audience, What real and lasting good has been accomplished by the advocate of temperance? Has there been any seed sown that will grow into the bud, the blossom, and the full-grown fruit? The subject of temperance, you are aware, is an old one, and our opponents have declared it stale, flat, and apparently unprofitable. It has been flung from the lecture-rooms in the land to give place to something more attractive, so that men who set much value upon their time and talents, avoid the advocacy of this cause as unprofitable. A life of devotion to any other calling is sure to bring profit.

"Labor and sacrifice to any other reform often secure a competency, and fling wide open the gates of social life. Under these circumstances, we have our reward in the consciousness of duty done. Is there any hope for the triumph of the temperance cause? Will time never scrape the inscription from the tombstones of this inefficiency? Ah! there is hope! I am always hopeful. I believe that the good day is coming, when it will be considered both respectable and fashionable everywhere to advocate the cause of temperance. I can even now catch the glowing inspiration of that golden age when this truth will universally prevail. When right shall triumph over passion and appetite, when the sickly sentimentalism that has taken possession of the morals of the people shall have been **cast** out, and a

pure love of humanity shall have taken its place.   Then
shall the Lord Jesus Christ be known and honored by
all men ; then the living God shall be cherished as much
as mammon is worshipped to-day.   I have faith in every
scheme for the amelioration of mankind, though thousands may perish in the struggle between right and
wrong, truth and error.   It matters not, victory will
come, quivering with the light of truth and justice !   Do
you think me too sanguine?   It will be so if our friends
pursue unwearingly the path of duty.   I believed that
slavery, long before the rebellion, would perish, because God never intended that man should be ground
down to the earth.   I had faith in the success of the
Union cause in the darkest days of our war.   This faith
never forsook me ; it flashed across my mind long before
the hour of victory ; its inspiration made me love to
sleep upon the frozen ground ; it warmed into life the
chilly atmosphere of my prison cell ; and it chanted the
requiem of heaven over the consecrated dust and the
unmarked graves of my fellow-soldiers.   It was the
strength of this great principle of faith that led me to
buckle on my knapsack when the tocsin of war sounded,
and inspired me to keep it on until I escaped from prison,
and once more caught a glimpse of the home I loved so
well ; and until, on the ninth of April, 1865, I saw Lee
deliver his men as prisoners to Gen. Grant ; — and then
I took it off, and returned to civil life once more.   But
I cherish that knapsack still.

    "But to return to our subject.   You may ask me what
delays this reformation in which we are so much interested.   The first reason is because the business of rum-

selling is a profitable calling. Money is made rapidly and easily, and when we attack the pocket of that class of men, they fight desperately, and do all in their power to retard our movements. While this business is so profitable to the seller, it is quite the reverse to the consumer; it destroys health, makes demons of men, and ruins both soul and body, and brings in its train both widows and orphans. Another reason is in the fact that law gives the business a color of respectability. It defends the vender in his so-called rights. The rum-seller is received into society, and elected to places of emolument and trust; his family is respected. What do the people seem to care for the source from which a man's wealth comes, notwithstanding the very ermine in which they are clothed smells of whiskey? Blackstone once said, 'Law is a rule of action, it is a good principle'; but if Blackstone lived to-day, and saw our legislation, he might change the definition a little, and might see a rule of action prescribed, prohibiting every man from interfering with the rights of rumsellers. Does not every legislature know that the use of intoxicating liquors is detrimental to the interests of the community, and still the statutory patchwork of laws regulating the sale of liquors, is not calculated to advance the moral and social interests of mankind. We need to elect by our votes men who will be true to temperance at the State House, as well as at the fireside. Every energy, every resource should be brought to bear in our cause. I maintain that every rumseller knows that it is a crime to traffic in liquor, and no one dares to fill a glass with the poisonous fluid and then go home to his family and

9

then kneel and ask the blessing of God on his business.
But our cause is God's cause, and we can pray in faith
for his blessing to descend on our efforts; all that is
good and noble responds to our work.

> " Our cause is like the cedar,
>   It knoweth not decay;
>   Its strength shall bless the mountains
>   Till mountains pass away,
>   Its tops shall greet the sunshine
>   Its leaves shall drink the rain."

"The great hope of our cause, however, is in the
education of the people by moral and religious efforts.
All can do something in this work. I recollect many a
bitter night when I have stood at the intersection of
Ninth Street and Broadway, N. Y., without a cent in
my pocket, and without a friend in the world, when
I would have been glad to have heard a kind, encouraging word. We should not forget that the most degraded
and fallen is an immortal being who will live on forever,
long after the sun, moon, and stars shall have faded and
passed away. I would counsel kindness for the unhappy
inebriate, and commiseration for his faults, for he is
dragged down and trampled under the hoof of a demon,
and his struggles against the bonds that bind him are
often long and desperate. Reach out your hands and
lift him up, throw around him the sympathy and paint
for him the bright future which is possible. No man
has sunken so low in the scale of human degradation as
not to be affected by your efforts, and when you see him
walking erect with manhood written on every feature
only a little lower than the angels, and in the image of

his Maker, and feel that you have been instrumental in thus raising him, the blessed consciousness of duty done and humanity benefited will be your reward. The inebriate never forgets the height from which he has fallen. In the darkest days of my dissipation I often remembered my home and the scenes of my childhood.

"In 1860, I found myself homeless and a vagabond, in the streets of New York. I was not always so. I stood, as many of these young men stand, thinking myself safe while I sailed smoothly on the river of moderate drinking. I never thought any danger could come from **my** drinking. Some of my friends entreated me to stop, as I do you. I replied, 'I will stop before it is too late.' Ah! how many a poor drunkard has said that! How have I cried out in the bitterness of my soul, 'O! that I had heeded the warning voice of friends long ago!' If you persist, you will stand where I stood, and may never be able to break the thraldom of sin and misery that will bind you soul and body. Turn, then, before it is too late.

"I have been called a fanatic, **too** much in earnest about this matter. Go, suffer what I have! Go, feel the iron enter deep into your heart; have wife, children, friends, and all that is dear on earth, torn from you, and then come and see if you can talk moderately on this subject. I would that my tongue might be touched as with a live coal from off the altar of God, that I might in words that burn, and thoughts that breathe, picture this evil. If it is fanatical to stand between the young men of the land, and dishonored graves, to help the weak to stand, to soothe the dying man who has lost all by this vice, to banish by my vote, voice, and influence the rum traffic from the streets, then am I a fanatic, and I glory in the title."

Before he delivered this speech he was intensely nervous and uneasy, remarking "that he never felt weaker, and never had such a dread of facing an audience as on this evening." After he had spoken in this strain for a few moments, he looked me in the eyes, and putting his hand on my shoulder, said, "Do you know what this feeling is?" I replied that I did not, except that he had been working very hard of late; and must be fatigued. "No, no; that is not it," says he, "it is an attack of my old enemy. He has been whispering all day to me like this. 'You need something to stimulate. Just a little will inspire you and help you,' and it is only by the grace of God that I am enabled to say, Get thee behind me, Satan."

But the large crowd that greeted and cheered him made him strong again, and the next morning, though much exhausted by his effort, he was cheerful and happy.

As that large concourse of people sat that night spellbound by his eloquent and impassioned words, which fell "like apples of gold in pictures of silver," little did they even dream of the mighty change that was soon to come over him. Now manhood was seen in his movements, and he seemed inspired by an angel. But alas! "Let him that thinketh he stand, take heed lest he fall." For no man who has ever been under the power of this appetite is safe, while this traffic in souls and bodies is carried on in every city and town of our nation under the name of the liquor business."

Thousands and thousands of drunkards reel through this country to-day, and nearly every one of them might be saved to God and their friends, if this business of "drunkard making" could only be stopped; but, while it goes on, seventy thousand of this staggering army will drop into dishonored graves every year, —while, reader, from your sons and daughters perhaps, the ranks will be kept full. How long, O how long, must this continue? When will we understand and comprehend the magnitude of this question? How many more hearts must bleed and break? How many more homes must be broken up and scattered? God hasten the glad day when our people, inspired of heaven, baptized with a spirit of devotion to humanity and their country, shall make the air of America too pure for a rumseller to breathe in, and our streets the highways of virtue and safety.

The following letter is quite significant when we remember what soon followed : —

" I never have been so 'used up' with my labors as now ; my friends all say I need rest, and I presume they are right, but you know how hard it is for me to give up when there is anything for me to do in the line of temperance. When I feel physically weak there is a whispering within me saying, 'Stimulate ; it will help you'; and I do not dare to give up my efforts in the temperance line, for I shall be more exposed to the attacks of my appetite. I confess I feel sometimes a little discouraged when I think of my own action — that

I have placed myself 'under bonds' during my natural
life, that I dare not do what others do, but still I suppose this is my cross, and I shall try and bear it; and by
the help of Him who was tempted in all points even as
we are, I trust I shall come off the victor. You know
he that conquers himself is greater than he that takes a
city. I desire in all confidence to tell you that I have
felt unusually despondent of late, and my appetite at
times has come over me with great power, and were it
not for many kind friends who cluster and gather around
me, I should almost feel like giving up the contest.
Were it not cowardly, I feel sometimes as though that,
God willing, I could lay down my earthly arms and enter
on that new life. How many of us would feel more so,
did we not have a dread of the 'unknown country' that
lies over the dark stream of death. I trust, however,
this gloomy state of mind is only temporary, caused by
my health, and in a few days I hope to assume my usual
good spirits.

"Last evening I had a glorious sail, and was on the
water when the sun went down, and I watched a little
while and saw daylight deepen into night, and gazing in
the direction of the east, I saw a faint streak of light;
and gradually it grew brighter and brighter, till the great,
round, silver moon began to come up, appearing like a
ball of fire rising out of the water. Did you ever see
the moon come out of the ocean? If not, let me tell
you it will pay you to come down here and see the grand
spectacle. How, I could not help thinking, as the moon
capped the waves with a silver tint, how many poor fellows sleep away down deep among the dark caves of the

sea.   And in that day when the trump shall call the
'quick and dead' to come forth, then from this grand
expanse of water those who have gone down to the sea
in ships, and have met storms that were too much for
them, and have gone down amid the roar of the winds
and the splashing of the waves, will appear.

"And I could but think how many there are in the
storms of life, who after fighting for a long while find it
too severe, and they have to yield and go down. We
don't know how hard the poor sailor fought before he
gave up his ship; perhaps he lashed himself to the mast
after he found he could not stand alone, and then I doubt
not he prayed to the God of storms for help.

"And O, my dear friend, how little does the world
know how hard may a poor fellow fights before he
gives up to the power of the temptation of life. Yes,
many a man has gone down like the Cumberland, with
flags flying and cannons firing. And the world speaks
of his yielding to his desire, when perhaps it was far
from his desire or wish. But I will not weary you. I
felt like telling how I felt, and have let my pen run
till I fear you will not care to follow me through all I
have written."

There is something about this letter different from any
other that we have read. And we cannot repress the
conviction that he had let the thought enter his mind
that he might have to give up notwithstanding all he had
endured, and the long time he had stood. Perhaps,
however, this may have been only a general survey of
those questions that were in his mind so often. There

have been those who have asked if he was not in the
habit of drinking occasionally when he was in the public
temperance work. We trust those who have read what
has been recorded here, are by this time well satisfied of
the utter impossibility of such a thing. If we could
close this story with this chapter, what a grand triumph
would it present of a man over a depraved appetite.
How would it encourage the men who have sunken low
in the scale of human degradation. But, alas! we must
with fidelity to our duty record the saddest part of this
changing life, and show how low a man may sink even
when he has risen higher than his ambition ever dared to
hope, for it may be said with all truth that at this time
Uniac was without a peer in the line of descriptive speak-
ers, with perhaps one exception. He was praised and
flattered on every hand, offers came to him to enter the
lyceum lecture-field, and in a financial view the induce-
ments were very tempting. One of the leading papers
of Massachusetts, in speaking of his last lecture previous
to his unfortunate trip to Connecticut, said: "It is now
some three years since this eloquent temperance orator
visited us, and we confess we were surprised and delighted
with the decided progress he has made; for, in beauty of
language, power of description, and impassioned eloquence
we have never listened to anything superior than his
effort last night. At one time the house would be almost
painfully still, and then worked up to the highest pitch
of enthusiasm. We hope we may soon be favored with
his presence again."

Thus on the highest round of triumph in the line of his
work we see this man to-day. But where shall we find
him to-morrow?

CHAPTER XIV.

CIRCUMSTANCES OF HIS FALL.

DURING the fall and winter of 1868 and 1869, Mr. Uniac was travelling and lecturing night and day in all kinds of weather, for he seldom failed to keep an engagement. In one instance he walked nine miles to meet an appointment; and arriving at the place of meeting, went on to the platform and spoke for nearly two hours, and returned afterwards to his room very much exhausted.

As might have been expected, this constant labor affected his health, and he began to show signs of breaking down. He complained of feeling weak and tired, and his friends advised him to take time to rest and recruit his energies; but his love for the cause of temperance, and desire to speak in its behalf were so great, that it seemed almost impossible for him to decline an invitation to lecture. When pressed for a reason for working when he needed rest, he said, "I feel safer from my old enemy when I am fighting him in the field of active work."

There is no doubt but what he feared for himself when he began to be in poor health, and thus kept on when he ought to have rested; for all reformed men tell us that they need the will that comes from a good physical condition to resist successfully the attacks of their foe. He passed through the winter of '68, and in the following spring spoke of taking a long rest; but his anxiety to help the cause induced him to accept engagements in March. Among the invitations received and accepted was one from an Irish temperance society in the State of Connecticut, for the evening of March 17th, to celebrate St. Patrick's Day in a rational and proper way. He had been informed that great preparations had been made for his reception, and he was so anxious to have a good lecture that he undertook to prepare a new one, all of the work on which was done at night, or between his other numerous engagements; and in the exhausted condition to which we have alluded, this extra effort was too much for him.

The day arrived for him to go, and found him quite unwell. He conferred with several friends as to the expediency of telegraphing the society to postpone the lecture, and was advised to do so; but after thinking the matter over, made up his mind to undertake to fulfil his engagement.

He felt the power of appetite as he had not for months, and went to several friends and invited them to go with him; but as he did not inform them of the great danger he feared from the power of his all-pervading appetite, and the weakness of his physical system, they happening to have other engagements, declined accompanying him. He was then recommended to take some quinine bitters, which was said to be good to build up and strengthen the system. On his way to the Boston and Albany depot, he stepped into an apothecary store and inquired for the quinine bitters. The clerk took down a bottle, and Uniac, taking it in his hand, said, " Do you know me, sir?" The man said, " Yes, this is Mr. Uniac, the temperance orator."—" Well, then, you know," says Uniac, "that I can take nothing that has alcohol in it ; have these bitters anything of the kind in them?" The apothecary answered, "Not enough to hurt anybody, if there is any. There may have been a few drops when they were first made put in to keep them, but still, know-ing you, I can cordially recommend them to you."

Uniac bought them, went to the depot, called for something to eat at the saloon there, and while waiting took a drink of the bitters, but did not like its taste, and leaving the bottle in the depot took the train for Con-necticut. After he had been in the cars a few moments, he felt a terrible craving for liquor, and feared the bitters must have contained alcohol. Arrived at the place of destination, the committee and others met him at the depot, and in the excitement he rose above his appetite. Without eating anything more, he went to the hall, found it crowded to repletion, and hundreds unable to gain admission, waiting on the outside.

He was received with great and hearty enthusiasm. After music and singing, he was introduced, and made one of the best speeches of his life. Many who had heard him several times before, reported that they had never listened to him when he was so eloquent and pow-erful as on this occasion. From the hall he went back to the hotel, several friends accompanying him.

He was conscious of a dizzy, sinking feeling, and while in this state, from the best of evidence, we are inclined to think that brandy was administered to him,—

probably from the best of motives, — for when he came
to, his head throbbed and he had the burning sensation
peculiar to men who have been drinking. He drank
water, but nothing seemed to quench his thirst. He
said to himself, "What shall I do? Would that I had
one of my friends here to help me!"

He looked at his watch, found a train was about due
for Providence, R. I., hurried on his clothes, took his
carpet-bag, ran for the depot, and arrived there, just in
time to take the train. He arrived at Providence too late
to connect with the Boston train, and there he was, in a
strange city, in this terrible condition, his aroused appetite continually crying, Give! Give! Give!

He walked backward and forward on the platform,
and then a few steps down the street, and finally entered
a store purporting to be a grocery store, for the purpose
of getting a glass of milk and a cracker. As he entered
he saw several men drinking whiskey. The air was
loaded with the smell of it. He struggled until great
drops of sweat stood on his forehead, but he was too
weak.

Some one who had been drinking, said, "That is
excellent whiskey, it makes me feel better."

Poor Uniac was gone; he grasped the bottle madly,
and filled a tumbler almost to the brim; draining it to
its dregs, called for more; for appetite had triumphed
and was now the master. He drank two or three times
before the train came, then filled a flask, got aboard the
cars, and started for Boston. How different from when
he left home! What a fall was there!

On the way his condition was noticed by several pas-

sengers; still it was not generally known in Boston for
several days. He went from Boston to Lawrence to see
a dear friend of his, and it was in the streets of that city
that he was first seen by the public intoxicated.

The next morning an item appeared in one of the Lawrence papers in regard to his breaking the pledge, and
in an uncharitable manner stated the facts in the case.

It was now all over with Uniac. His friends at Lawrence did all they could for him, but to no purpose. He
came back to Boston in disgrace, and spread consterna-
tion among his friends, and caused sorrow and heartfelt
pity wherever he was known.

The news ran like wildfire. Every newspaper told a
different story in regard to his life and fall. Uniac
opened his heart, and with tears in his eyes told his
friends the awful story of his fall as given above, which
has been corroborated by unimpeachable testimony, so
that it may be relied on as correct in every particular.

His friends now rallied around him, and every possible
effort was made to reclaim him. Letters poured in from
every quarter, urging him in behalf of the cause to begin
anew, and promising assistance of all kinds; but now,
having broken the spell, the struggle was fierce and desperate. It was finally decided to take him to the Wash-
ingtonian Home, in Boston, where he remained for a
little time; but feeling that if he could be farther removed
from old associations, he would be more successful in his
efforts to reform, he concluded to go to the Inebriate
Asylum, at Binghamton, N. Y., then under the charge
of that skilful superintendent, Dr. Albert Day. He
started, accompanied by a friend, reached New York

without much difficulty, but while there had another
drinking spell; but through the firmness of his companion, he was finally prevailed upon to leave New York.

He arrived at Binghamton the next morning, and was
immediately placed under treatment at the asylum.   Dr.
Day expressed the hope that he would soon be master
of his appetite, and stand erect and firm; but he had a
dreadful ordeal to pass through, as only those who have
had the same experience can understand or appreciate it.

While there, letters continued to come to him from all
parts of the Union, and, to show how he felt at that time,
we will give a letter that we received from him, in reply
to one sent there.

BINGHAMTON, N. Y., 18—.

"DEAR BRO., — Your kind letter of sympathy and
encouragement is received.

"It is as I expected. I thank you for your kind
words, and did you know how I fought ere I yielded,
you would not blame me as much as I fear some do. I
have begun the fight anew, and by God's help shall continue it while life lasts. I have often told you that my
life was a struggle, but I never felt more determined to
live and to die for the right than now.

"God bless all my friends for what they have done for
me, and I know you will excuse me for not writing more
at this time, as I am very weak.

"Fraternally yours."

Other friends received letters of a similar character,
all regretting what had taken place and hoping for the

best. The reader will notice the struggle comes out here, so that it can be seen and almost felt.

When we consider to what heights he had risen as a public speaker in the short space of four or five years, and see what countless numbers of friends he had, his fall was indeed one of the most remarkable in all the history of the temperance reform, and the cause of it must be indeed powerful.

We can seem to understand how a disappointed, disheartened, poverty-stricken man may take drink to drown his sorrows if he has this appetite; but why a man like Uniac, with everything in life bright and hopeful, and a future aglow with happiness, should take that into his mouth which should utterly ruin and darken that future, is a mystery which can only be solved by admitting the power of appetite as something uncontrollable. Rev. Theodore L. Culyer says, in the "Independent" of May 20, 1869, "It is nearly thirty years since my beloved friend, the unrivalled ——, first appeared before the public as a reformed inebriate. He has been doing ten men's work ever since, and has addressed more auditors on both sides of the Atlantic than any living orator. With what a terrible emphasis does he warn his fellow-creatures against a single sip of the intoxicating glass! 'I *hate* it,' he often exclaims, with furious vehemence; 'and I *love* to *hate* it!' Yes, my noble brother, although a faithful member of Christ's church, is 'under bonds' for a lifetime, to keep out of the sight, sound, or smell of spirituous liquors."

What shall we learn from these facts? Shall we abandon our efforts to save the victims of intemperance? No!

we must leave no means untried to lift up the fallen. But one of the real lessons to be learned is to save the young from ever contracting habits of intoxication.

This is the great hope of the reform. If the question, Shall the coming man drink wine? is answered in the negative, this country is indeed safe. If in the affirmative, then will the foundation stones of our government be unloosed, and the fair fabric of a grand republic totter and fall! In every part of the land men are tramping in solemn procession to drunkards' graves, and if we are not able to prevent those who have already started, we can surely hinder others from joining them.

There is also an unanswerable argument in the fall of this man, in favor of the principle of prohibition; for who shall say after reading his life, devoted to an almost constant struggle in trying to free himself from the power of rum-drinking, that he would have sought for it even at this time of desperation, if it had not been flaunting itself in his very face. Suppose in the city of Providence where he first took liquor, the prohibitory law had been as well executed as it is in the city of New Bedford, in the State of Massachusetts, where it is almost impossible to purchase a glass of any kind of intoxicating liquor, because the municipal officers are elected and sustained on this issue, Uniac would probably not have fallen; and hundreds of others, situated as he was then, would stand, were it not for the fact that on every street corner, in windows and on shelves, are displayed in the most tempting manner these fascinating drinks.

When Uniac entered the store to get something to eat, suppose it had been a temperance saloon, and he had been able to get what he entered for, it doubtless would in a measure have relieved him till the spell had passed ; and knowing that he could not procure liquor easily would also have given him strength and power.

Hence, while we may found and endow asylums for the drunkard, and throw around him the circle of friendship and love, we shall never save our country from intemperance, till we enact in every State in the Union a law prohibiting the sale of liquor, which shall be enforced by men who have been elected for the purpose of doing this important work. But while many men who profess to love the temperance cause, and who talk long and loud for three hundred and sixty-four days in the year, and on the other (election day) walk to the ballot box **and** deposit their votes for men who will betray the cause into the hands of its enemies, we cannot hope for much real improvement in the moral condition of our large towns and cities.

But when principle and not party shall be the rule of action, when men shall begin to fully comprehend the responsibility God has put into their keeping in the matter of securing a wise and honest government, and an honest administration of the laws, then shall we see this land emerge from the cloud that hangs over it, and our people, if true to themselves, be a blessing to mankind, and the country an honor to the world.

The fall of this man who had been so prominent in the temperance reform created discussion all over the country, and it might be amusing, but perhaps not profitable, to read the different versions that were published in the newspapers of the day. Some who were not friendly

10

to the cause doubted his sincerity, and claimed he had
not been faithful for a long time, while others declared
that the cause came from disappointment in this or that
direction.   One paper said the recent loss of money was
the occasion for the immediate fall, and in. fact all kinds
of stories were presented to the people.

A religious paper of New England, in referring to the
work of rum at this time, truthfully said, "The most
eminent newspaper man Boston ever produced, so far as
business tact and success goes, died lately in the prime
of his life, a victim of intemperance ; the most popular
temperance lecturer, with one exception, that this sec-
tion had ever known, has fallen a victim to his appetite.
Those two losses answer all the miserable talk about
liberty and right to thus murder the souls and bodies of
men.   What thousands on thousands of cases belong to
the same catalogue?   Can any one doubt the duty of
the State to save its children?   But for the bar and the
wine tables of the hotels, those gentlemen would be in
life and honor.   How long, O Lord! how long !"

Dr. Albert Day, the skilful superintendent of the inebriates' asylum, at Greenwood, Mass., tells us that the
general effect of excessive drinking, is to enlarge globules of which the brain, the liver, and other organs are
composed, so that the globules, as it were, stand open-
mouthed, athirst, inflamed and most eager to be filled.
Everything within the drunkard gapes and hungers for
the accustomed stimulate.   Dr. Day says he has known
the old appetite, even after twenty years of strict abstinence, burst out in full force, simply from the medical
use of a little wine.   According to this testimony, from

a man who had devoted his life to the study of this matter, we account readily for the fall of Uniac.

However much we may debate the cause, we say with
Cuyler, " Let the doctors and debaters say what they
will, the verdict of common-sense is, There is no safety
but in total abstinence, and that from childhood."

The great point now with our subject, and with all
those who loved him, was to have him regain his lost position. It is not an easy thing to recover the confidence
of the public in a matter of this kind, for a very little
thing would create talk and speculation. And he, being
by nature impulsive, did not seem to have the patience
to work his way slowly back into the hearts of the people ; he seemed rather to desire to leap with one stride
back to his former position, and felt discouraged because
he could not. We shall not forget the occasion of our
first meeting, after his fall. We met, and taking each
other by the hand, neither spoke for a moment, when
tears began to run down his cheeks, and he trembled all
over like a leaf. I was the first to break the silence,
and gradually he became calmer, and proceeded to give
me a detailed account of his misfortune. If ever a
man showed sincere sorrow for an action, this man did
for his false step. After conversing with me for some
time, he said, " Well, I only know what I must pass
through to place myself where I stood a short time ago,
and I pray God to give me patience and perseverance to
continue until the end." Yes, I thought, poor fellow,
you must indeed have patience and faith, for the fight
will be a hard one, and the result uncertain. Some people
do not see how it is possible for a man who has re-

mained sober for years, to go back to his cups, through
the power of the old appetite. But there are too many
instances on record for us to doubt the truth of it. I
remember one day I had the pleasure of dining with a
man who has been a total abstainer for nearly thirty
years, and in conversation on this point, his wife remarked : —

"Why, my dear sir, though it is nearly thirty years
since my husband signed the pledge, I would not dare to
place on my table even preserves, if in their making
there had been used never so small a quantity of wine or
brandy." Turning to him I said, "Do you also fear that
after you have controlled your appetite for so long a
time, that such a small quantity would revive its power?"
"My wife has not overstated the matter, for even now
I have days when there comes over me a desire for drink.
You see, sir, it is impossible to ever forget the peculiar
sensation of this powerful agent," replied he.

We often see merchants going into intemperance after
they have met with some financial trouble, but in nearly
every case, the habit of drinking had been contracted
long years before; while the cases are very rare, where
men, who have been total abstainers from their youth
up, ever fall into these habits, though they may meet
with even worse disappointments.

Thus a man who has at any time been intemperate, is
in continual danger of being pushed into the rapids of
despair by the power that he first admitted voluntarily into
his system. When this question shall receive the attention its importance demands, — when the children in our
schools shall be educated and informed as to the true

character of alcohol, — cases like the one we are here recording will be indeed rare, for after all the discussion of the temperance question for the last forty years, it is astonishing how many people we find who have not the slightest conception of the power of alcohol. Some people seem to look at the matter as of small consequence, to be stopped at any time when it shall be thought best, when it perhaps might take a generation for the evil effects to die out, if we should prevent the further use of the beverage to-day.

But "Uniac has fallen," and these words have fallen with a crushing weight upon many a heart, and the deepest concern is manifested that he shall be saved. Letters pour in, asking if anything more can be done to help him.

The following touching letter from a man Uniac had been instrumental in saving will show how men of **this** character felt about this sad matter.

My DEAR UNIAC, — Had I been struck with a blow from heaven, beneath a clear sky, I could not have been more stunned than I am by the news that has come to me that the enemy of your life has got the best of you.

"O, my dear brother, I can never forget the day you came to my home, and helped me to stand; how your presence seemed to brighten our home; how my wife had once more a smile on her face; how our dear little one was happy again, and all the world seemed to grow better and better, and you, my staff, my hope, and almost my savior, has gone down where I was for so long a time. O, let the memory of the good you have done in homes like mine, inspire you to beat back the enemy, lash him under your feet, and stand up in all your glorious manhood. Let me remind you of the night I heard you lecture. I was induced by my wife to attend. I went ragged and dirty, bloated and miserable, and the words you spoke seemed to thrill my very soul; and as you spoke of a chance for all to become men, I saw for the first time for years that it was possible for me to be a man. And when I signed the pledge, and you took my hand, and to encourage me came to my home and told me your story, and for two years I have been a sober man. And now you have gone down. O, I cannot write, for the tears blind my eyes. God help you to stand, is the prayer of one who loves you like a brother.

          " Affectionately yours,

                     "B—— H——."

Doubtless this letter was of service in the contest, for written on the back of it, were these words, "Is it possible that in my fall I may carry down men like these? God forbid; I will gird myself for a decided victory."

We will follow him in his efforts and see the result.

CHAPTER XV.

DESPERATE STRUGGLE TO REGAIN HIS FORMER POSITION — LETTERS, ETC.

AFTER remaining at Binghamton for a short time, he was anxious to return to Boston; uneasy in his present condition, he now felt that he could gain faster among his friends. He was advised to remain under the care of Dr. Day for a longer time, but he decided to return, and did so.

This was the latter part of March or the first of April, and as his course about this time is familiar to nearly all the temperance public, it will not be interesting for me to give it here. To say that it was a daily and hourly struggle for weeks and months is to tell the whole story. Sometimes he would be sober for two or three weeks. He had been sober for about three weeks, when on Friday of the week before the Peace Jubilee, we noticed that about him which led us to suppose he was having an unusual fight with his appetite. We were now with him almost every day and night, and it was arranged that we should stay by him. I slept with him that night. In the morning he got up before I did, said he felt stronger, and was going to the Boston and Maine Railroad depot, to meet a friend. The next I heard of him was that he had been seen intoxicated on the street, and after searching for him through the day and evening, found him at a saloon in Haymarket Square. After some persuasion I induced him to accompany me to a hotel.

The remainder of the week from this time was the most disgraceful of all his career. As during this time Boston was full of people from all parts of the country, his condition became widely known, and some of his professed friends seemed to abandon him to his fate.

Matters went on in this way until one morning I received a note, saying a man in the police station desired to see me. I hastened there, and found the prisoners had gone into court. I went in, and looking into the dock, among that array, with all kinds, I saw Uniac ; his face bloated, his eyes blood-shot, hair dishevelled, clothes torn and dirty, and a look of utter despair in his eyes. As he caught sight of me, tears started down his cheeks, and he trembled and cried like a child. We succeeded in arranging matters with the court, so that he was discharged on a probation of six weeks, and from there he was carried to the private asylum, kept by Mrs. Dr. Fletcher, at No. 5 Asylum Street, of whom we had heard as an able and efficient doctor in this line.

She received him cordially, the best room in the house was placed at his disposal, and here he began, under favorable circumstances, to renew the struggle for life, character, and happiness. Under this skilful treatment, he soon began to mend, although very sick for about two weeks. When, in company with his medical attendant, he called upon me, he seemed to feel that this was his last effort, and he often said that if he fell again he should not live. When we said to him, " Why, you do not mean to say you would take your own life?" Stretching up to his full height, and looking me steadily in the eye, he said, "No, I am not such a coward as that; for though this fight is a hard one, I shall try and do my duty, leaving the result with God."

He improved now rapidly, and grew strong and decided; everybody who knew him and valued his services was pleased and hopeful. We cannot, however, with fidelity to truth, omit to mention that there were some *professed* temperance people, who, instead of helping him, did everything to irritate and discourage him ; such as falsely accusing him of drinking, doubting his sincerity, and parading before the public his private and sacred affairs ; all of which to a man in his condition were peculiarly irritating and uncomfortable ; and as the consequence he was often discouraged and disheartened. It is not our purpose to attempt to prove that Uniac had no faults, that he did not often give his friends occasion for sorrow and even distrust. He was human, subject to all the frailties that flesh is heir to, but the facts in his whole career will prove that his life was not a common one, and that he had within him that which tended to drag down and debase him, the appetite for strong drink, which is being fed and strengthened to-day all over our country, by men who for money are trying to sell the future virtue and glory of the nation; and if this story, the facts of which are stranger and more thrilling than fiction, shall help arrest this tide of intemperance, it will at least have accomplished something, and the death of Uniac will not have been in vain.

He now began to receive invitations to lecture again,

and consulted with his friends in regard to it, and was
generally advised to begin work as soon as he felt
strong enough to stand. Now was perhaps the most
trying position for him; with a keenly sensitive nature,
he could hardly bear the humiliation that came over him
as he faced for the first time after his fall an audience;
but he succeeded well, and began to be hopeful, and
anxious to do something to help himself financially.
Although when he fell he had quite a sum of money, he
was now very much reduced, and in many instances, while
under the influence of liquor, pawned his watch and
other valuables; but in this extremity he was not without noble-hearted friends who came to his aid with offers
of pecuniary assistance. John B. Gough sent his check
for a hundred dollars, and told him to draw on him for
what he needed.

Mr. Wm. B. Spooner, Rev. Wm. M. Thayer, James
H. Roberts, and others assisted him in like manner, and
it was the overwhelming and almost crushing thought
came to Uniac of what he had been, what he had lost,
and his dependent position, that staggered him and made
him doubt his ability to regain his lost standing. From
this time on he grew stronger, and was regarded as once
more himself. He spoke in various parts of the Com-
monwealth; but still, from what his medical adviser
stated, the struggle was at times fearful.

Every friend of temperance seemed now to be interested in the struggle. One evening, Mr. Gough was
speaking at Music Hall, and alluded to Uniac as follows: "There is a case now published before us in the
newspapers, that ought to excite the sympathy of every
true-hearted man.

"It is of a man that four years ago I saw in Camp
Convalescent, a soldier fighting the battles of his country,
but a slave to intemperance. I spoke in the morning,
and I spoke in the evening to the soldiers.

"I asked, 'Who is that young man?' and I was told
that he was a lawyer who had spent a fortune of forty
thousand dollars, and was one of the worst drunkards in
the regiment. That man signed the temperance pledge.

"I remember that my wife who was present with me,
said to him, 'Be of good courage, and may God
strengthen your heart in this fight.' And he fought it
for week after week. He fought that battle four years.
I have no doubt that every day it was a struggle. I
have no doubt he never saw the sight of drink without
wanting it. I believe he has some affection for me; I
know I have for him. He sent my wife a letter about
ten days ago, — a letter that would draw tears from the
eyes. He says, 'You have been a true friend to me;
Mr. Gough has spoken kind words to me. He ought to
know it. I have fallen.' Fallen! Ah, who can tell
the struggle in which he fell. How he was exhausted
by labor, when he fainted away from his effort to do
what he could, time after time for the advancement of
the interests of temperance, and save the poor victims
of this vice. And now he has fallen. Fallen? Uniac!
No, it is not fallen! Uniac shall come up again, by
God's help, and stand the noble man he is. My home
is open to him when he chooses to come, and he shall
come there when he likes." All this shows the power
of the awful appetite for drink.

In this connection, through the kindness of Mr. Gough,

we are permitted to publish several very interesting letters.

"No. 5 ASYLUM ST., BOSTON, July 20, 1869.

" JOHN B. GOUGH, Esq. :

"*My dear Friend*, — I am boarding and receiving medical treatment at the above number, the place now selected for me, and recommended to me, or rather to Rev. Wm. M. Thayer, by our mutual friend, James H. Roberts, Esq.

"It has been a home to me thus far, and I greatly desire to remain under treatment from which I have derived so much benefit. I have had no home since I broke my pledge, until I came here. I had a furnished room in the Studio Building, but it was a lonely place for a sick man. I was under constant excitement. I could not stay in my room, so I slept at the hotels here and there, and I made my way down *lower*, *lower*, *lower*, day by day. Those whom I had heretofore considered friends, seemed to shy me and the past. The tongue of slander grew loud. I saw but the black side of every picture, and I resorted madly to the bar, to drown the current of unpleasant memories. My health, too, was completely shattered. Physical strength gone, — self-respect almost gone, friends leaving me on every side.

"Hope, yes hope, that stays longest, was almost gone.

"Despair seemed to chase every hour with the race-steed of destruction. I felt that I was alone ; you will understand my struggle. You have passed through it, you are the victor. God knows it ! He has seen me, he has pitied me, and I feel confident that he has not only heard the prayers of others in my behalf, as well as my own faint, feeble petition, but that he has answered them. Have you lost all confidence in me?"

"Boston, April 19th, 1869.

"Mrs. Gough, — My good friend, your husband, first induced me to sign the pledge. I wish to sign it to him, and for him, again. His words have given me strength; he says he loves me, and his conduct proves it.

"He wanted me to pledge myself when he saw me here. I would not do it. I am sober now, and have been for a few days, and I desire that this news should be conveyed to him as speedily as convenient, for I know how much I grieved him when he was here; you will please forward it as soon as you can, for I feel that he is anxious about me.

"And now what shall I say? How can I thank you for the deep interest you manifested in me when at your house? O, Mrs. Gough, you will pardon me for causing you so much trouble. I did not know what I was doing. I have taken the doctor's medicine regularly up to this day, and I believe it has helped me greatly.

"Will you please remember me to your family, and believe me to be your deep debtor and attached friend.

"P. S. You told me to look to God for strength. I have done so, nor have I looked in vain."

"BOSTON, April 19, 1869.

"JOHN B. GOUGH, ESQ.

"*My Dear Friend*, — Your cheering words at Camp Distribution, in 1864, flung the first glimmer of hope into my heart. I signed the pledge, and began the battle. It has been a fierce one. O, how fierce, God alone knows. The kindness of yourself and Mrs. Gough at that first interview made you very dear to me; that, and every victory I have gained since that time, has increased my love; you were my friends then, I find you still unchanged. To you I come on this day, by this letter, clothed in my right mind (I have not drank since Tuesday), to renew my pledge before God, and in your presence, never to touch nor taste again, even as a medicine. Oh! Mr. Gough, you have been a true friend to me. I will need your influence now, as I never have before.

"Beginning once more with nothing but hope, and a few friends that God has left me, it will be a hard struggle. I will pray long, and fight desperately. God will not forsake me.

"Affectionately, your stricken friend."

We are also permitted to give the following beautiful letter : —

"BINGHAMTON, N. Y., April 6, 1869.

"MRS. KEITH,

"*My Dear Sister*, — Your favor of yesterday is at hand. It finds me in the enjoyment of perfect physical health. I have received a very large number of encour-

aging letters, many of them from parties from whom I
least expected to hear; but they have not been able to
'minister to the mind diseased.' The seam across my
heart is open, and bleeding as fresh to-day as it was the
very day that I entered this place. Nothing that I have
yet received has in the slightest mitigated my trouble,
or alleviated the pang. The light by which my hope
walked six weeks ago, shines no longer. I have become
the harbinger of secrets that I wish I never knew. I
distrust myself, and for the simple reason that I know of
those whom I would trust as soon as I would trust my
own soul, and yet I find my character assailed by them,
when I am not in a position to defend myself. All that
friends can know of me in the future, they must learn
from other lips than mine. I know the danger of this
resolve. It involves conjecture, and conjecture always
magnifies.

"Of course I am calm, but it is only the calm that
mantles the hour when storms have passed away. It is
only the calm of a volcano after some frightful eruption.

"You have stood on the beach and watched the waves
roll up, until their curling crest broke and died away.
While trembling from the shock, the waves rolled back
again, gloomy and sullen. So have rolled, rolled the
waves of my life. The appearance of the storm and
anger has passed away, many of the clouds have melted
off,— even some sunshine has come in, much of it appears without; but I state the fact, when I say that I
never before felt so much like a frightened snail, curling
itself within itself.

"My mail since I came here has been very large, so

that I have had to devote my entire time to letter writing,—and now many of my correspondents are still neglected.

"I leave here during the course of the week. . . . It would be an old story to say that I was glad to hear from you,—of that you are always assured. I will endeavor to write to ——, as she requested, but I don't know that I can find time. You will please remember me in love to all, and believe me to be, as ever,

"Your brother."

Though many of his friends had a good deal of confidence in him, those who knew him best saw how keenly he felt the disgrace; feared it would be doubtful if he ever entirely regained his former position. Through the kindness of James H. Roberts, Esq., of Boston, we are able to give the following interesting letter, which shows how hard he labored to help him; and gives a good idea of his condition at the time of which Mr. Gough spoke at Music Hall.

"DEAR SIR,—In answer to your letter I would say, that Mr. Gough lectured on the subject of Temperance in the Boston Music Hall, April 13, 1869, when he feelingly referred to Mr. Uniac's fall, and paid a noble tribute to his labors in connection with the temperance cause.

"At the close of the lecture, Mr. Gough was informed that Mr. Uniac was in the hall. A messenger was despatched, who soon returned with him. He was very much affected and wept freely, although at the time under the influence of liquor. We took him to the Quincy House, where Mr. Gough plead with him a long time, as no other man could have done. He would not absolutely promise to abstain, but said he would try. It was arranged that I should take him to Mr. G.'s house, where he should spend some time in quiet, under the influence of that noble family. At this time, Mr. Uniac was very sensitive, and would not allow me to accompany him home. He was so persistent, that I left him in a horse-car about half-past ten, P. M. He agreed to go directly home, but the power of appetite was so strong, that he again yielded, and spent most of his time that night in a bar-room at the south part of the city, arriving at Mr. Keith's between two and three o'clock in the morning. The next day he was confined to his room, and suffered very much from exhaustion.

"On the morning of the fifteenth, I started with him for Mr. Gough's. I was told by a gentlemen who had taken an interest in Mr. Uniac (and had had much experience with inebriates), that he must have some wine when we arrived in Worcester, as it would be impossible for me to take him to Mr. G.'s without some stimulus. When we arrived at South Framingham, he wanted drink, and he was so determined to have it, that I was obliged to use force to prevent him from leaving the car. On our arrival at Worcester, he was very weak, and on the verge of delirium tremens. His constant cry was for drink, and he declared he should die without it. I took him into an apothecary store, and gave a light dose of cherry wine. I went to order a carriage, leaving him with my friend, Mr. Mecorney, and, upon returning,

11

found he had escaped. I soon discovered him, however,
in an oyster saloon. We then started for Mr. Gough's
house, five miles away. He begged for more drink, and
declared that he should die before reaching our destination, unless it was procured for him. He was in a very
bad condition, and remembering what was said to me
before leaving Boston, I stopped at an apothecary store
and ordered a rather light dose of wine, the small quantity displeasing him very much. On our arrival at Mr.
G.'s we were received very cordially. He appeared
much better. But Mrs. G. not being able to give him
the constant attention which he needed, and Mr. G. away
from home, it was decided that he should return with
me. We stopped some hours, however, and Mr. Uniac
appeared to be much improved. She gave him medicine, and he ate quite a hearty dinner. On our departure,
she gave me a letter to her family physician in Worcester, in which she explained Mr. Uniac's case, and he
prescribed for him.

"We called at the store of Mr. Mecorney, in the post-
office building, and while standing in the door talking
with Mr. M., Mr. Uniac desired to drop a letter in the
office which I had just written for him. Not knowing
that there was a back entrance, I thought there was no
danger of his escaping. Still I kept my eyes on him, saw
him drop the letter in, and noticed him attentively scanning the boxes, occasionally looking at me; but he did
not appear to have any disposition to leave. He finally
stepped into a recess, and was out of sight. I at once
started for him, but he eluded me. I went to the rear
door, but he was nowhere to be seen, and it appeared to

me that no man could have accomplished such a feat, even in an attempt to save life itself. Mr. Mecorney and I started in pursuit, travelled the city over, visiting all the places where he knew liquor to be sold, but could get no tidings of him. We were about to give up in despair, and thought of putting his case in the hands of the police, when Mr. M. proposed looking in an apothecary's shop, where he believed liquor to be sold. We found no one present, but upon entering the *back* office, found Mr. Uniac there with two or three others. He was very much intoxicated, and he told me that he drank eight times in that place.

"It was now six o'clock, and there was no other train until 10.30. How to pass the time for four and a half hours, with a man so much intoxicated, was a question not so easily answered. I walked with him in the street for about one hour, then took him into a restaurant, and ordered a bowl of strong beef-tea.

"Having partially quieted him, we went into the theatre, there being no other place of entertainment. Securing seats on the lower floor, he remained quiet during the first act. He then becoming restless, I took him into the balcony, and tried to interest him as well as I could. He requested me to leave him alone, which I did, taking a seat only a short distance away. At the close of the second act, I requested him to go back to our former seats, but he refused to do so, stating that I must leave him alone. He remained in the dress-circle, while I went to look for our overcoats, which we had left below.

"I sat down in full view of Mr. Uniac, and my close

watch annoying him, he changed his seat, taking one
a little farther back.   He would lie down on his
seat for a moment, out of sight, and then look up and
laugh, as though he were playing with me.   This he
repeated several times. ' At last, losing sight of him
longer than usual, I started for the balcony, but he had
again escaped from me.   I left the theatre at once, and
went into the nearest bar-room, which was under the
Bay State House, and there I found him, just putting the
glass to his,lips.   I spoke sharply, and told him that I
had lost all confidence in him.   He appeared to feel
very badly, wept like a child, and said if I could not
trust him, there was no use of his trying to reclaim his
lost position.   I talked plainly, telling him, if he did
not try, I should, and that he could not have any
more drink.   He gave me one of his defiant laughs,
and said he would have it if he lived, and that I did not
know the cunning of an inebriate.   I told him if that
was the case, he would not live, for he should go to
Boston, dead or alive, without liquor.   For two minutes
he looked me in the eye, as only a drunken man can,
and that glance will never be effaced from my memory.
At length, with his eyes still fixed on me, he said, 'Do
you mean that?' I answered firmly, 'I do.' He said,
in a subdued tone, 'I am ready to go.' We then
started for the depot.   He was very calm, and did
not ask for more drink.   I became more and more
convinced that it is folly to try and sober a man by
giving him the lighter drinks.   If I had not heeded
the advice given me in the morning, the result might
have been different.   I have referred to this day's trial

to show the desperation of the man, and the means resorted to, to obtain drink. He slept most of the way to Boston. Mr. and Mrs. Keith were expecting us, as I had notified them by telegraph that we were on our way home.

"Soon after this Mr. Uniac was taken to a private asylum, where he remained till his death. I saw him often, and no man appeared to try harder than he to reform. I entreated him to go back in the country and remain quiet, believing as I did that he needed rest. As he was financially embarrassed, I offered to pay his expenses, to which he would not consent. During the summer I gave him all the money he needed, and in fact all he wanted, but it was in small amounts. His board was paid promptly, and usually in advance, so he was not embarrassed by that. Mr. Gough instructed me to give him one hundred dollars on his account, which I did, and Mr. Uniac gave Mr. G. his receipt written in his peculiar and feeling style.

"Mr. Uniac was a man of more than usual power, — generous, impulsive, very sensitive, quick to resent a slight, but nevertheless a true friend. The more one associated with him, the better they would like him. He did not appear to have the firmness or strength to resist his powerful appetite. He seemed to be conscious of this, for on several occasions he had been known to invite friends to accompany him, for the sole reason, as he would afterwards acknowledge, to protect him from yielding to temptation. Although a victim at last to his appetite, he nevertheless, by his earnest, eloquent appeals, accomplished much; and his words

of warning to old and young will not soon be forgotten."

This letter gives a good idea of the condition he was
in many times between the hour when he fell in the city
of Providence and the time of his death.   There are other
friends who could present similar instances of those desperate spells.   In referring to his feelings when going through
these ordeals, he would say, "Don't place any confidence
in what I say when under the control of appetite ; for a
man will deceive or do almost anything in order to satisfy
the demands of his inordinate desire for stimulus."   In
what Mr. R. has so graphically related, we see this truth
manifested in his attempts, by deception, to get out of
his sight and hearing.   When this man was sober, his
word was not doubted by any one, — showing that this
yielding to appetite takes the honor and manhood
out of an individual, and leaves him poor indeed.

He had, as stated before, so far recovered his former
strength as to go into the field occasionally and labor ;
but usually some friend went with him, as he felt safer
and better to have company.

One night he was to lecture a few miles out of Boston,
and called on a friend to accompany him.   They left the
depot at six o'clock, and arrived where he was to speak
at about seven o'clock.   The meeting was to begin at
seven and a half ; and, after being introduced to the
committee, he appeared very uneasy and restless, getting
up and walking across the room, going to the door and
returning, and in various ways exhibiting signs of
nervousness.   Just before the time to go to the hall, he

said, " I will step outside a moment "; saying to his friend,
" You remain here." But this man knew him too well,
and followed him at a little distance, saw him hurry
along, and occasionally stop and look to see if he was
observed. After going the length of two or three blocks
he was just stepping into a saloon, when his faithful
friend put his hand on his shoulder, and said, " Where
are you going? " With a look that plainly told that he
was about to drink, he said, " O, my dear sir, if you
suffered what I have since we left Boston, perhaps you
would do what I would have done had I got inside of yonder door." He was reminded of his engagement to speak,
and that it was nearly time, and this seemed to turn his
attention in a new channel, and he entered the hall.
He was received with a good deal of enthusiasm, and
made the following remarks, and it will be seen that
his feelings, suggested by the above instance, showed
themselves plainly in his speech.

" MY FRIENDS : — I wish I could unfold to-night my
real condition. I wish I had the power to lay open to
the young who are here my crushed and wounded heart;
I feel it would be a better temperance lecture than any
words of mine can make. I am laboring under a peculiarly heavy burden of body and spirit, and I only am
here through the earnest entreaties of my friends. I
have often thought perhaps I had better not attempt to
occupy a position on a temperance platform, for my life
is not such as to make it entirely sure that I shall benefit
the cause. But God has seemed to point this as my
duty, and **so I am** glad to be here, for it is one of the

grandest things a man can do, to follow out his duty.
Some men I know are deceived as to what is their duty,
and plod on, through a weary life, entirely out of their
correct line of action, never rising above a low level;
while, should they turn their talents into that work
which their abilities are fitted to perform, they might
rise to grand heights of excellence; but that it is the
duty of each of us to live in our moral natures in such
a way as to honor God and help our fellow-men, no one
can for a moment doubt.   And how little do we seem
to understand and appreciate the responsibility that God
has put upon us in regard to our influence upon our
fellows.   'Am I my brother's keeper?' ought to sound
in our ears night and day, until we see how far we shall
be held responsible for the future of our weaker and
yielding friends.   I need not spend time here to-night
in attempting to show that the man who puts the cup
to his neighbor's lips is injuring and perilling all his
future, as well as making bitter the pathway of those
who are near and dear to him by the tender ties of love
and affection.   I know you will excuse me to-night if I
refer to myself somewhat, for some of the acts to which
I shall allude cannot be better illustrated than by my
wasted life.

"Suppose when those who professed to be my real
friends saw, as they must have seen, that I was of a
social nature, that if I continued in the way I had started
I should sink low in the scale of humanity,— I say suppose
they had then used their influence in the direction of a
pure life by abstinence from foolish indulgence and an
earnest effort to better the condition of those around

them, my whole life would have been changed for the
better without a doubt.   I tell you, young man, though
you may be strong, though there may seem to be no danger from the course you are pursuing, let me tell you
there is some one upon whom your life is having an influence, who perhaps is weaker ; and while you stand, you
will see him going rapidly past you towards a drunkard's
grave, and the blood of his life is on the skirts of your
garments.   O, when will men awake from this selfish
sleep that holds them ! — if I am only saved, is all that
concerns many people of this age.   I know men in some
of our towns who are the leading persons, — honored
and respected, — who are drinking moderately, and forgetting that by this act their influence is being felt, and
will show itself in the after lives of some of the boys of
these towns.   What makes me a slave of my appetite?
What made me wander up and down the streets of New
York homeless and friendless?   It was that having tasted
and loved the contents of the 'cup,' the habit was
encouraged and kept alive by the influence of men who
lived honored and respected, and some of them have died
lamented by the community, — while only by the grace of
God, and a continual battle to keep down my appetite, shall I be able to keep from filling a drunkard's
grave.

   "If we were all formed by nature alike, with the same
desires, with the same firmness and decision of character,
with the same weakness, — then he who went down
would alone be to blame, and on his head would be all
the responsibility.   But while I am weak in this regard,
while one glass of this fire will set me all aglow with a

burning fever, and carry me on till I sink to the lowest
place on earth, and a man by my side drinks·the same,
and stands, and looks at me with contempt, — I tell you,
sir, by every law human and divine, he should abstain,
and thus by his influence help me. You may not all
agree with me in this logic, but, sir, when you have suffered what I have since the fatal day I took that to my
lips that awoke the slumbering appetite, when you have
seen life through only the darkest clouds, when you
have carried in your bosom a heart as heavy as mine,
when you have seen the hopes of a lifetime dashed to the
ground, — when you have seen and felt all this, you will
perhaps see this matter in the light that reveals it to my
eyes. 'Total abstinence for the individual and prohibition for the State' is the only rule of action that will
safely carry you and me through this life.

"If the prohibitory law was rigidly enforced in every
town and city I enter, I could walk the streets with
safety ; but to-night, because it is not, I came near being
lost again, and had not a friend, who has watched me as
a mother does her child in the moment of peril, rescued
me, I would not have had the pleasure of looking in
your faces a sober man. When I received an invitation
to be here to-night, your committee will remember I
wrote I hardly dared to promise I would come, for I was
not fully confirmed in my ways of soberness ; but, God
helping me, I will strive to win back the confidence of
those who have done so much for me. Let me, in conclusion, ask you to awake to new energy and life ; remember the men like me, who need your help and sympathy ; think of the homes you can brighten. And

never forget that all can do something. No one is so
humble as not to be able to unite in this work. One
night, after a terrible battle, a little drummer boy went
with me over the field where lay the dead and dying.
Some were wounded near unto death, and we could not
hope to do anything but try and smooth their way to
the other world; as we found so many needing help, it
was indeed painful to hear the cries for assistance. I
turned to the drummer boy, and said, 'Can't we do
something to relieve these men?' And he said, 'O,
yes, sir; I am bringing water from the cool spring yonder, and bathing the lips and aching heads of these dying soldiers.' And sure enough, there he was, running
from one to the other, with this cool, health-giving beverage, trying to soothe and comfort these patriots. As
I saw what a little thing this was in itself, and how
much comfort and good it was doing, I felt that there is
no place on this earth where we cannot do something
for the good of others.

> "'Let us, then, be up and doing, with a heart for any fate,
>   Still adhering, still pursuing, learn to labor and to wait.'"

The above must have been among the first of his
speeches after his fall; and while we cannot put into it
the impassioned eloquence of illustration and power of
delivery, we can form some conception of how this
struggling man felt as he stood on that platform that
night.

When he reached home that evening, something sooth-
ing was administered, and he fell into a pleasant slumber
and in the morning awoke feeling calm, and stronger
than for some time before.

He continued to improve rapidly, and began to speak frequently in various parts of the State, to the acceptation of the people, — many remarking that he seemed to throw a new life and power into his words and thoughts, while at the same time there appeared to be a kind of a gloomy shadow resting on his life. His attempts to be cheerful were easily seen to be forced, and his nearest friends regarded this as one of the worst features of his case. Still, hope for the best led them to do all in their power to cheer and make glad his way, and many a heartfelt prayer went up to God in his behalf.

CHAPTER XVI.

CIRCUMSTANCES OF HIS **DEATH — SPEECH — EXTRACTS**
FROM **DIARY, ETC.**

HE had now been a sober man for nearly four months,
and had greatly improved in health and appearance. It
was arranged to have him accompany me on a lecture tour
through the towns beyond Fitchburg, in the northwestern
part of the State of Massachusetts. Everything being
ready, he called at my office on the morning of Oct.
10th, at nine o'clock. We were to leave at eleven, **and**
before going had some conversation in regard to his
condition. He said, " I have to a certain degree regained
my former strength. Still there is an indescribable sensation comes over me at times causing me to look at everything with a gloomy feeling, and it is with considerable
effort that I am able to shake it off. But while I have
hours when it seems as though I must yield to my appetite again and go down forever, I am much better than I
have been at any time since my fall in March." We left
Boston soon after this, and, during our long ride, he
appeared cheerful, and discussed the question in regard to
whether this power of appetite was a disease, something
which we must doctor the patient for, or whether it was
a habit which was under the control of the will entirely.
He presented arguments to prove it had something to
do with the free choice and desire of a man, but was not

clear about what it came to be in the course of years of
indulgence. While engaged in this discussion we were
pleasantly interrupted by a gentleman who introduced
himself as an old comrade of Uniac. For a moment Mr.
U. did not seem to recognize him; when his identity
flashed across his mind, he cordially shook him by
the hand, and for nearly an hour they spoke of old times
when they camped, marched, and fought together. I
well remember how sad Uniac's face grew as he said,
"Well, my dear boy, I am indeed glad to see you, but
what I went through in those days are not to be compared to the sufferings and sorrows of the last six months.
You know after I signed the pledge, and began to fight
the appetite for liquor, I told our company one night in
a speech, that, God helping me, I would never touch or
taste a drop of liquor while I lived; and, George, I meant
what I said, but I had no conception of what an awful
contest I should have to go through." The soldier
cheered him by kind words, and left us at the town
of Fitchburg. After taking a lunch we rode on,
and reached the town of Gardner about four o'clock, and
were met at the depot by one of the committee, and
escorted to a pleasant and comfortable house where we
were to spend the night. In the evening, although it
stormed, the Town Hall was crowded, and Mr. Uniac
made an eloquent and powerful speech. In the course
of his remarks, he referred in an humble way to his fall,
and though he spoke with some confidence as to his
hopes for the future, several at the close of the meeting
remarked that there appeared to be a solemn and shadowy
cloud about what he said, as though cheerfulness and

hopefulness were feigned. After receiving the congratulations of the friends who had come out to hear him, we returned to our room and talked of the past; he reviewed his mistakes and failures, and said, "If we would only be guided by our *past* mistakes, our future would be free from a good many things that had impeded our progress in the days gone by." When we came to retire, he took from his carpet-bag some bromide of potassia, which he said he was taking for the purpose of quieting his nerves, and making him sleep. We asked him if he knew the nature of the drug, and he replied that it was very simple; but from the quantity he confessed he was taking regularly, we told him we feared it might injure him, and he concluded he would begin after this trip to reduce it.

We had seen so much of him since his fall that we felt it to be a duty to exercise the greatest care of him, and when he left the room for a few moments, we examined the contents of his valise, and felt sure he had nothing else that he was taking. He slept well during the night, and on awaking, we found it to be a very stormy day. He was to speak at the same hall, should the weather prove favorable this evening, as he lectured in the night before. We kept our rooms nearly all day, and he was not out of sight except about an hour in the morning, when in company with the gentleman who was entertaining us, he visited the factories of the place, in which he appeared much interested.

After dinner, he complained of being sleepy, and laid down on the bed, and slept so long and soundly, that we aroused him, and inquired if it was the medicine that

made him sleep so; he made no reply, but continued to
be very drowsy and sleepy until nearly time to attend
the meeting, when he aroused himself, went to the hall,
and found it full of people who were members of the
order of Good Templars, who had come from all the
towns in the immediate vicinity. His speech was one
of his best, being of a descriptive character, in which
line, it is well known, he excelled.

Nothing unusual occurred that night, except I could
not fail to notice the change that had come over him
in the matter of being sleepy, for it was with considerable difficulty that I awoke him in the morning; and
while he was dressing himself, I again inquired if he had
not something else with him to make him sleep. He
evaded the direct question, but gave me to understand he
had only the bromide of potassia.

We were now carried over to the town of Temple-
ton, and arriving there took rooms at the pleasant hotel
of the place.

We were to speak that evening in the Town Hall, and
he expressed a desire to remain in-doors, refusing an
invitation to walk after dinner. He had one or two
callers, and spent the rest of the afternoon in sleeping.

In the evening a good audience greeted him, and he
seemed inspired by the occasion; and as this was the last
speech I ever heard him deliver, it is written on my
memory in letters of an indelible character. And I will
give some extracts which the reader will see partake of
the sadness of which we have spoken.

"We have met here to-night under pleasant circumstances, — pleasant and yet sad to me, for while I have

been sitting here, my mind has been wandering backward. I do not forget the time when in this vicinity I had the honor and pleasure to meet many I now see, but then how different. O, what a change has come over me; why, I have seemed to live a lifetime in the last few months, and only by the mercy of God and the efforts of dear friends, I am here. Our relations in this world change often, but there are few changes that ever come over any man's life so marked as that which came near putting out forever the light of my soul. But, my friends, through all the darkness that shrouded my being, I never forgot the kind friends who were praying for me all over the country. I tell you, if I never appreciated friendship before, I value and prize it now; for by this storm that has beat against me, I have been able to separate my real friends from my professed ones. When the sun is shining, when nothing obstructs the way, then we see certain people flocking around us. When there is something for them to expect, all is well; but let a cloud, though it be no bigger than a man's hand, appear in our sky, and you see these people begin to give you more room. But if I have seen a few of this kind, thank God I have seen many who, as the darkness grew more and more intense, would draw closer and closer until they would shield me entirely from the pitiless storm. I will not name those men and women, but in the book kept by the good angel, I doubt not their names are written in letters of light.

"My friends, men who stand as I did, need help; they need encouragement, not for a day or a week, but all the time; they want to feel that there are some hearts that

12

beat in sympathy and love for them. You cannot begin to appreciate this, unless you have passed through some such experience.

"I remember when after my fall I began to think of my condition and realize how my friends would look at my act. While thus musing, a hand was placed on my shoulder, and a cheerful voice said, 'My dear fellow, what can I do to help you?' Turning around, I saw it was one of my best friends. I could hardly speak, for his words had touched my aching heart; and from that hour to this, that friend, and many others, have stood by me, and God knows I can never be thankful enough for what they have tried to do.

"My dear friends, let me entreat you, by your love for this cause of God and humanity, to stand by the weak and tempted men all around you."

He then discussed in an able manner the issues of the hour, and presented a picture of surpassing beauty when the evil of intemperance should pass away.

In conclusion he said, "I have detained you longer than I intended to, but I never go on to a platform to speak now, but the thought comes over me, perhaps I never shall have the opportunity to address these men and women again, and I desire to leave on your mind one thought. It matters but little to the world, perhaps, what may become of me. I have tried to do all in my power to help the cause of humanity; that I have failed in doing my whole duty, none knows better than I; but the thought I wish to leave here is that, whether I stand or fall, live or die, I am sincere in my desire and efforts to do right. I have never yielded to temptation only without struggling and fighting long and well, and though I have not been able to stand erect all the time, God knows I would be willing to sacrifice anything I have, for the sake of this glorious cause. I mean to live and die fighting for it; and whatever may be in store for me or you, I implore you fail not to do all you can to help men who to-night are yearning and dying for kind words and tender acts. I may not ever meet you again here on earth, but O, let us so live, that when we are called upon to lie down, to give up the mortal, we may put on an immortality radiant with brightness, and mid the flowers that grow by the river that flows fast by the throne of God, meet and sing forever."

There is nothing remarkable about the above extracts; except, as I took them down in my book, and read them over after his death, they seemed to be so full of his heart-language, that we felt that to all who knew him they would be interesting.

At the close of the lecture, he was informed that it would be necessary for us to arise in the morning as early as half-past three, to take the stage, in order to get the first train for Boston, which we felt our duty to do.

In the quiet of that night, we talked of all he had passed through, of his hopes and fears, and, taking my hand, he said, "You and other friends have been kind to me; I trust I shall be able now to stand." The tears gathered in his eyes, and giving my hand a firmer grasp, he continued, "God only knows how hard I am fighting, and what I endure." We encouraged him as best we could, and he went to bed. He was, however, very restless and uneasy, arose several

times, fixed the fire, and consulted his watch. From
the time we took the cars till we reached Fitchburg, he
slept soundly. At this place we met a friend, and
Uniac engaged in conversation with him, till we reached
Boston. Arriving there about nine A. M., we went
directly to a restaurant on Tremont Row, where he ate
a hearty breakfast.

We then saw him home to his residence, he desiring
us to do so; for I think he had some fears he would
not be able to reach there without some trouble, as it
would be necessary for him to pass several places where
he had often drank when under the influence of liquor.
He had agreed to spend the next Sabbath at Lawrence,
and being very much exhausted on Friday evening, the
day he arrived home, he wrote that he did not feel able
to come, and begged to be excused. On Saturday, he
remained most of the day in his room at Asylum Street.
On Sunday, Dr. Richards spent part of the day with him,
and his medical attendant noticed nothing very unusual
in his appearance. He seemed in fine spirits, and need-
lessly communicative in regard to himself, stating things
at the dinner table which were calculated to depreciate
him in the minds of some people. But self-justifica-
tion was not one of his faults, and concealment was
contrary to his nature. Monday passed as usual.
Tuesday he called on the Rev. J. B. Dunn, told him it
was four months since he had drank any liquor, and
seemed happy and pleased that he had resisted so long.
His faithful attendant told us, however, that he was
more or less alternately depressed and excited, and that
now she felt sure he had begun to take something of

the nature of opium; and, feeling so sure of this, on Wednesday she took measures to counteract its influences.

On Thursday he was to have gone to Vermont to lecture, but in his bad condition it was not thought prudent to have him undertake the long journey alone. He, however, for almost the first time, objected to having any one go with him. He was allowed to sleep as long as possible that morning, and then aroused. He was late, and dressing himself hurriedly, started with an attendant for the depot, but reached there about ten minutes too late to take the only train that would reach the place in time for the lecture. He was very weak and nervous, and this disappointment excited and annoyed him exceedingly.

He kept taking bromide of potassia, and from the best authority that we are able to procure, we find he had taken during this day eight or nine times of this medicine, but had not drank any liquor up to now, and was fighting desperately the final and most awful struggle of his life. Who can estimate or understand it? Those who saw him twenty-four hours before this last fall, could but feel that he was going through a severe and doubtful contest. He had grown thin and pale, his nervous system was completely shattered and broken down; and the opium which he doubtless took was taken for the purpose and in the belief that it would aid him in the effort to stand. His friends were faithful and untiring in their efforts to help and save him. Some one of them followed him every step, and watched over him by night and by day.

Thursday afternoon he demanded liquor; he coaxed, begged, and threatened. Finding his condition such that unless some was allowed him he would become unmanageable, his attendant reluctantly consented to let him go out, on his promise that he would immediately return. He took his hat and went to the nearest liquor-shop, and unfortunately for Boston, be it said, he did not have to go far before he found one. It is, however, but justice here to say that it is more than doubtful whether he could have been prevented from leaving the house by those then with him, even had the attempt been made.

When he got inside the saloon, he probably drank freely. At any rate, his condition showed that he had indulged to a considerable degree. He also procured some whiskey in a bottle, and brought it to the house, where he arrived as soon as he had promised.

No one knew but himself the amount of opium he had taken previous to this, but probably more than he intended or knew the consequences of.

It was now near evening, and he began to show signs of being very sleepy, and soon fell into a sort of stupor, but he came out of this in a short time partially, and asked his medical attendant to remain and watch with him during the night. After answering a few questions in an unintelligible manner, he fell into a heavy sleep. Almost immediately after this, the attention of the watcher was attracted by heavy breathing, which she knew came but once, and that immediately before death.

Medical assistance was now summoned, and everything done that was possible to relieve and help him. But, alas! the fight is almost over, the man is too weak and far gone to resist much longer. While those around him were watching his every movement, he roused himself sufficiently to inquire where he was, and then immediately sank back. He opened his eyes once more, and after gazing around the room with a kind of vacant stare, with some difficulty lisped a name that had been sacred to him in brighter and happier days, before the storm-cloud of sin and intemperance had overwhelmed him, and then gently fell into that sleep whose awakening is in Eternity.

The struggle now is ended, the victory over the man complete. All is calm; no more tears, no more struggling days and nights, no failures nor temporary victories, but peacefully and serenely he rests, though vanquished and conquered by his life's enemy.

Tell me, ye who profess to judge men for a course the cause of which you know nothing, has this man's life borne nothing but leaves? Has this life been all a failure? Has it not borne buds and fruit that will open and ripen white and beautiful just over the river in that garden where flowers bloom but never fade?

Who can stand by the side of this tenantless clay and say, "Had I been he, I would have resisted this power"? Who can say at the close of life, "I have done all I could"? That he fought nobly, the record of his life shows; and God the Saviour and Father of us all knows the harvest of his life. Though dead, he speaks eloquently to the young men of this age with a warning voice that ought to penetrate every heart, to avoid the evil that was his curse and destroyer.

The are few instances in all history of men who have

been before the public so short a time, who have become
more widely known, and more generally loved and
respected than Uniac. By his own exertion he placed
himself almost at the head of descriptive orators in the
space of four or five years, and his power and eloquence
have been felt all over the country.

Mr. Uniac had read a great deal, and could repeat for
hours together from the standard poets, without making
a mistake. His memory in this particular was truly
wonderful. A lady writing from the western part of
Massachusetts, says that one evening after the close of a
lecture she concluded to test him in this line, and said
she took from her library nearly all the English standard
poets. She would then open the books at random, read
a line, and in nearly every instance he would take up the
verse and carry it along with surprising accuracy. For
nearly two hours she tested his memory in this way,
and she remarked that it was beyond belief to find what
a store of reading he could repeat. We have the testimony of men of culture who have associated with him
as regards his reading, and all pronounce him one of the
best-read men of the times, considering his opportunities.

It has been thought by some people that Uniac, finding himself too weak to stand before the world an upright, sober man, took the opium with the intent to end his
days ; or, in other words, committed suicide. We confess,
at first this did seem reasonable, but after the reflection and
investigation we have given the circumstances, and from
letters in our possession, we feel certain this was not the
case. It is true after his fall on the 17th of March, when
he had become sober again, he did say to several of his

friends that if he went down again he should be a dead man, or words to that effect; but from a letter written just before he died, we find he must have meant by this remark that he thought he would not be strong enough to stand another fall, for he was not like many who drink, taking it sometimes moderately, but when he had once tasted it, he continued to drink fearfully day and night. In the letter of which mention has been made, he says, "I do not think if I go down again, I shall live through it. I do not mean by this that as much as I would like to flee from the sorrows and temptations of this world, I would do such a mean and cowardly act as to commit suicide; for that is indeed unmanly, and unworthy of any sane person; but I fear my strength will give out, and my system be unable to stand the strain that comes when I give way to my appetite." In another letter he refers to the same matter as follows: "Amid all my sorrows I never was so mean as to contemplate getting rid of them by taking my own life." We may therefore safely conclude that he died fighting. He felt that the opium would *aid* and give him quiet and sleep, and being in a terrible condition from his efforts, he took more than he intended, which, together with a large quantity of bromide of potassia and the whiskey, caused his death. He was not strong, for we know that when he was placed in the asylum where he died, he was very much reduced in strength, and never seemed to fully recover from the attack of sickness he then had. It will be difficult for us to find a man anywhere who was all his life (after he found himself a slave to alcohol) apparently trying to reform, and so often under such agony of spirit and body. Those who have seen him as he contended, and heard him cry out in the anguish of his burdened heart, "O my God, must I live and die a drunkard?" know he was in earnest, and know he went down fighting. And though he made a desperate stand, we can only say that his enemy was stronger than he, and won in the battle.

The following extracts from his diary, written during the same month of his death, will show how his heart felt, for we have been impressed with the tender personal matter we have found written here, which none but God and he ever saw.

"I am heartsick to-day. I wandered down the street this afternoon, and as I passed some of the places where I have had liquor, I felt some unseen power urging me to go in. Will I ever free myself from this feeling? Shall I ever stand secure again? I tremble when I think of my ever again yielding."

"I am better this morning, and am to try and speak this evening. Some of my friends feel it will give me strength to see an audience, and feel something of their inspiration."

The following was written after the lecture. "I had a good house last night, and feel much encouraged. I went this P.M. over that portion of Boston that is cursed by a large number of rum-shops, and as I looked at the little boys and girls who in their faces and forms showed that the evils of intemperance had been inherited by them, and then saw men standing behind bars, pouring out this vile stuff that had made all this misery, I felt that the 'golden age' we often speak of is yet a long way off, and I **offered** up a heartfelt prayer, as I gazed on the doings of rum, that I might escape the terrors of **a** drunkard's life and awful death."

"I have only time to write a line in my book, to record the 'old, old story,' my 'appetite has been very strong all day.'

"I am to go on a lecture tour. I must have rest and sleep, or I shall not be fit to stand before an audience."

"One more day of my life has been recorded by the angel of time, and I am still a sober man; by God's help I am enabled to say this. It seems as though it grew harder for me to keep my feet in the right path, for every day I have to fight."

The following are the last lines we find penned, and were probably written when he had made up his mind he must yield or had yielded. He only begins a sentence, and abruptly closes without finishing it.

"Darkness has come over me, my light has gone out, I can only — "

These extracts seem to confirm what has been said about the motive which led him to take the opium. In his case he seemed to have spells or periods, when he would have unusually hard times to stand firm against the demands of his appetite, and when he wrote the above he was going through one of these periods. When he wanted sleep, while off on the lecture tour, he must have taken it, and when he returned to Boston increased it; it had the effect to intensify his desire for liquor, and while under the influence of this drug he took the liquor, and after the excitement of the opium had subsided, the other effect came over him, and caused a sleep

which knew no waking. A spirit of unrest is seen in the
few extracts above, and perhaps had his physician been
aware of his true state he might have been helped; but
he would often put a good face on his condition, and thus
deceive those in attendance.

But he has gone to that place "where the weary are at
rest, and the wicked cease from troubling." No more will
temptation fret and harm his peace, for he has passed over
the river and is beyond the reach of injury from those who
have caused him, and those who loved him, so much sorrow and misery; but we cannot forget that there are
hundreds and thousands of others who walk our streets
trembling with fear for themselves, and those about
them.

Reader, as you look into the faces of your little boys,
and kiss them good-night, remember Uniac once played
beneath the green trees of his home, and at his mother's
side repeated his morning and evening prayer, and went
out from her sight pure and innocent. And because of
the temptations that were set for his young feet, he had
a life of struggles and an untimely death. Would you
make the future of your boys safe, instil in their young
hearts a love for the temperance cause, early at the altar
of total abstinence swear them, and, by example and pre-
cept, help them make their future. But, doing all this,
there will be some of them who will lose the influence of
your home education, and come under the power of other
associations. And if you would make them safe, you
must, by your actions as citizens of this free country, close
up the dram-shops, and all that follows in their train,
and by the strong arm of the law enforce obedience to

the principles of virtue and temperance, for true liberty consists in doing that which shall in no way interfere with the rights and privileges of others. And no man or set of men has a right to place before the young men of our country that which has ruined thousands, and will continue to ruin as long as it is allowed to be sold.

In the name, then, of Uniac, let us gather new inspiration to fight on beneath the temperance banner till victory shall crown our efforts.

CHAPTER XVII.

FUNERAL EXERCISE — SPEECH, ETC.

On the 28th day of October, the friends of this gifted man assembled in the Beach Street Church, the Rev. J. R. Dunn, pastor, to pay their last respects to all that remained of a man dear to many of their hearts. The day was wet and gloomy, and nature herself seemed to be in mourning for the occasion.

Many men of distinction from the various walks of life were present, to show that though he had often disappointed their just expectations, still the good he tried to do, and the effort he made to be true to himself, entitled him to respect and honor.

The casket that contained the remains was covered with the choicest flowers, that had been tastefully and beautifully arranged by the loving hands of friends who knew and appreciated all the tender and lovable traits of character which this poor unfortunate man so often displayed to those near and dear to him.

Seated near the body were some ten or fifteen children from the Orphans' Home, where Uniac had often spoken words of kindness to the motherless and fatherless children whose little hearts so often ached to hear. The services were held at the noon hour, and just as the tones of the tolling bell had died away, the orphan children came forward, and taking each other by the hand, sang in a sweet and feeling manner an appropriate hymn; at its conclusion the Rev. Mr. Edmonds read some selections of Scriptures, and prayer was offered by the Rev. Dr. Chickering. After which, the Rev. J. D. Fulton, D.D., of Boston, was introduced and made an eloquent speech, spoke of the failings of this poor brother, and held up his death as a warning to all who were tampering with the contents of the wine-cup. The Rev. D. C. Eddy, D.D., then addressed the people.

He came down from the pulpit, and, standing by the side of the coffin, spoke touchingly and tenderly of the "poor, gifted, weak, and tempted brother," as he called Uniac, and said, "I do not know which to speak of, this man's faults, or his virtues; his failures, or his successes." He alluded to the bitter struggle of a lifetime; told of the hours this man had stood with the enemy under his feet, and showed how active is the enemy of virtue,— for in an evil hour when the brother was physically reduced in strength, at just the right time he comes in on him like a flood, and overcomes his strength."

He then eloquently enforced the lesson of the hour on the young men who were present. "Uniac," he said, "speaks to you to-day from out his coffin, in a manner that cannot but impress you; far more eloquently and powerfully does he thus speak as he lies there with his lips closed in death, conquered by intemperance, than he ever spoke when in his grandest and best days." After relating a few instances of a personal nature, in connection with what he had seen of the man while he was trying to save himself, he concluded by saying, "Let this

lesson be heard and heeded all over our land, and Uniac
will not have lived and died in vain."

The Hon. Henry Wilson being present, now came forward and spoke a few moments. He began by alluding
to several occasions when he had met this " poor, struggling young man" trying to stand, told of some of his conversations with him, and how on one occasion the tears
ran down Uniac's cheeks as he tried to show him it was
possible for him to regain his lost position. He then
spoke of the power intemperance was exerting all over the
country, and related in the most eloquent manner some
instances of the work Uniac had accomplished. He told
of an instance when he heard him speak, and said he
regarded him as a young man of great promise. Mr.
W.'s remarks were tender and feeling in their nature,
and when he had concluded, there was hardly a dry eye
in the house.

After the singing of a hymn by the audience, the
Rev. J. B. Dunn made the closing address. Mr. D. had
been peculiarly near the deceased since he began in the
temperance work, and therefore his remarks were of
such a nature as to make them very interesting to all who
were present.

He began by referring to the good and tender heart
this man had, and how he made himself one of your
dearest friends, if you knew him long. He spoke of the
last visit he had from him, and how cheerful he seemed,
and also told of the many times he had seen him when
his appetite was fighting for the victory. No report of
this speech or in fact of any of those given on this occasion,
can do anything like justice to them, for the entire ser-

vices were of a solemn and impressive character. At the close of the exercises an invitation was given for all to take a last look at the face of the dear departed; and that large concourse of people slowly walked by the coffin, and many an honest, heartfelt tear was shed above this man's remains on that sad day. When the friends had all passed, we followed all that was mortal of Uniac, and laid him in the soldiers' lot at Mt. Hope Cemetery, where he sleeps to-day, peacefully, side by side with those who had gone forth to battle for our country. And every year, to the sound of solemn music, the comrades of these brave dead march, and with uncovered heads strew their graves with sweetest flowers. Should the reader ever visit this sacred spot, perhaps he may feel like shedding a tear above the grave of a man who saved by his work and power many a poor victim of intemperance, but, alas! could not save himself; for what this man tried to be, — for what he was enabled to be to the cause of temperance for five years, — let us never forget, or cease to love, his memory. And while we may find much to condemn in almost any man's life, when we remember the circumstances that surrounded Uniac, we will not hastily judge him.

13

CHAPTER XVIII.

LETTERS FROM REV. WM. M. THAYER, REV. E. P. MAR-
VIN, D. D., REV. W. H. H. MURRAY, WENDELL PHILLIPS,
HON. HENRY WILSON, REV. GILBERT HAVEN, D. D., REV.
D. C. EDDY, AND J. H. ORNE, ESQ., ETC.

WE have the honor and pleasure of presenting in this chapter letters from some of the ablest men connected with the temperance movement, and they show how highly the subject of this book was held in the estimation of men of this character.

The first one is from the pen of the Rev. Wm. M. Thayer, of Franklin, Mass., Secretary of the Massachusetts Temperance Alliance, who was perhaps as well and intimately acquainted with Uniac as any other person, and was held in high esteem by him.

"DEAR SIR,—I am glad to hear that you are preparing a memoir of the late Edward H. Uniac, Esq., so well known to the temperance public. No one was more intimate with him than yourself. You knew him in private as well as in public, and hence can but appreciate those personal qualities which endeared him to so large a circle of devoted friends. He was one of those rare young men, who must be seen in the private walks of life in order to be known. In his nature, delicate as 'a harp

of a thousand strings,' so sensitive that even a mild crit-
icism would bow his soul as a windy storm bends the
forest, it was not strange that he often felt this to be a
hard world to live in. You know, as well as I, how
many sad, sad hours he passed, because of the fearful
appetite with which he had to battle. And when, after
four years of valiant struggling against the demon-power
within, during which he thrilled the hearts of admiring
multitudes by his eloquence and burning thoughts, he
yielded in an evil hour, and fell, you know the agony
of his spirit. You can never write it in a book, — poor
human language is inadequate to express it.

"Never shall I forget that first interview with him after
his fall. I had loved him almost as a younger brother,
and the tidings of his relapse had filled me with honest
grief. We met, — he the poor, fallen, trembling victim
of rum, and I his friend and brother. You may well
imagine the rest. There were no words. With locked
hands, emotion was more expressive than words. His
whole frame shook with feeling, and told what a hell of
bitterness had opened within him.

"It seemed as if his whole fleshy tabernacle were falling to pieces, from the power of emotion within. I have
often said that I never saw a man so convulsed with
anguish as he was.

"I was often with him during the three months that
he was under a cloud, sometimes standing up nobly in
the contest with a raging appetite, and sometimes returning to his cups again.

"I was with him when he was in his right mind, and
when he was not.

"Again and again I went with him to the throne
of grace, where he felt that his only hope was. He
talked and prayed like a Christian. And when once I
went to him in my plain, blunt way, and told him that I
wanted more proof that he had a Christian hope, that
the scenes of the last few weeks had shaken my confidence in his cherished hope, he only wept, and assured
me that my confidence was not shaken more than was his
own; and wished to bow with me again at the throne of
mercy, adding that if 'God's help is not vouchsafed,
my case is indeed hopeless.' The last prayer that I
heard him offer was at my family altar.

"It was humble and penitent, expressed in a simple,
childlike manner, with a tone unusually subdued. Afterwards he asked me if I did not notice how difficult it
was for him to give utterance to his desires in prayer.
On replying that I did not, he seemed surprised, and
added in substance, 'I feel so unworthy that I am
almost dumb when I try to pray, and often I feel that I
have no right to express a Christian hope.'

"'But you do not relinquish your hope,' we said. He
signified that he did not on the whole, though he hoped
with many fears. My whole intercourse with him confirmed me in the opinion that he was a Christian. We
know not how much allowance to make for such a case as
his. 'No drunkard shall inherit the kingdom of God,'
but he did not die a drunkard. You and I know that he
was sober for four months before his death, and bid fair
to rally and be useful again,—that he did not die in consequence of returning to his cups, but died in a desperate effort to prevent a return to his cups, by an overdose

of laudanum. The world can never know the fearful conflicts that he waged with appetite. There may be more virtue in those contests, in the sight of God, than there is in the total abstinence of men like you and I, who never knew the appetite for strong drink.

"Uniac was a brilliant man. In some respects he was the most remarkable man I ever knew. His wonderful command of beautiful language made him a fine conversationist; while his knowledge of classic writers, particularly the standard poets, contributed very much to make him the centre of attraction in the social circle. His memory was remarkable, and he would repeat more extracts from standard authors than any man I ever knew. The wife of a clergyman who is very familiar with the English poets, told me that she once tested him, by reading extracts from the different English poets, when he would immediately tell which author she was reading.

"His affection was like that of a little child, gushing and overflowing. It was called weakness by some. Perhaps some misconstrued it, because of its familiar, intense character. I admired it in him, because it was in keeping with his other qualities. If half of the men had some more of woman's loving nature in them, the world would be much better than it is.

"Uniac was not perfect: who is? He had his faults: who has not? Much of his life was wasted in sin; could not God forgive him? He died 'under a cloud,' but some clouds have silver linings.

"I loved him while I knew him, and now that he is dead, I cherish his memory.

"Yours truly,

"WM. M. THAYER."

The following is from the Rev. E. P. Marvin, D. D.,
of Wellesley, and is touchingly beautiful :—

" WELLESLEY, — 1871.

" DEAR SIR, — You ask me for some recollections of
our dear friend Edward H. Uniac.

"I was not very long acquainted with him, and saw
him only in his grandeur. He is a mystery in my thoughts.
I recall him as great brightness and sudden darkness.
He came in sight like a gallant ship, which, sailing up the
horizon as if borne on wings, and is suddenly arrested by
an unseen and inexplicable tempest with which it battles and struggles for a time, and then goes down in
horror and gloom.

" I never knew which to admire most, Uniac's voice,
his graceful manner, or his ready thought and language.
Doubtless it was the finely balanced combination of all
these, and the powerful interaction of each of them upon
the others that made him almost incomparable.   He told
me that it was the louder tones of his voice alone that
roused him before an audience, and set his mind and
imagination in full play.   He said he could do nothing in
a small hall, or to a small audience, comparing it to
speaking out of a bung-hole ; but when he heard his voice
pitching and rolling like the waves in a storm, then all
his powers awoke, and he could say what he had never
studied out or dreamed of saying.

" At such times the lofty and grand strides of his mind
seemed to me like the march of an angel from mountain
top to mountain top.

" The same voice, moderated to the family and modulated to the repeating the choicest portions of English poetry, we have known to charm, and hold spell-bound whole social circles, from the youngest to the oldest, for hours together, with the power of the æolian harp.

"His kindly feeling, his sense of honor, and his generosity knew no bounds. He would gather all the friends he could, and draw them to the refreshment table to regale them with viands and conversation; and when he entered with them, with lifted hat and graceful bow on all sides, he was the centre of attraction, and the cynosure of all eyes. These same qualities, when he was in temptation, rendered the battle with his great enemy more fearful; and the knowledge of these enlarges our charity in judging him.

"The account which I at first received of his former dreadful life, his reformation and conversion in the army, given me by a ministerial friend and chaplain, was most affecting, and established me in the permanent confidence of his real Christian character, notwithstanding the darkness of his departure. No Samson dies in vain.

"Who can tell but that, in the wise and deep orderings of divine Providence, even the strange, sad close of a career, with such brilliant opening and promises, may be of more value to the cause of temperance and humanity, than even his life could have been? Never was there a more telling example of the unconquerable and deadly power of the drinking appetite, nor of the inexorable necessity of legal interference, to save the fallen and to close up the alluring ways to the seductive appetite, which surely brings in its train poverty, shame, wide suffering, and dreadful death."

Now follows one from Rev. W. H. H. Murray, of
Boston, which will also be read with interest.

"BOSTON, Feb. 9, 1871.

"DEAR SIR, — Uniac was a most unfortunate man.
He was not properly organized for defence against that
power which was ever assaulting him, and which at last
overcame him.   His life gave daily evidence of many
noble qualities.   He made friends as easily as a flower.
In thought and act he was fragrant with courtesy and
kindliness.   He broke impetuously, as it were, through
the barriers of your reserve, and took your heart by
storm.   But the very warmth of his nature exposed him
to peril.   With a cooler temperament, with a more cau-
tious and self-controlled nature, he would have been
better equipped for the battle he was called upon to
fight.   As a warning to all gifted and ambitious men,
his memory is more eloquent even than were his words.
If you shall be able to present him in your work 'true
to the life,' you will at once pay a just tribute to the
nobility of his character, and prolong the influence which
it was the aim of his ambition to strengthen.

"W. H. H. MURRAY."

The following is from Wendell Phillips, Esq. : —

"DEAR SIR, — I knew Mr. Uniac, and am glad you are
writing his memoirs.   Such a life has a deep interest,
and especially just now, — one of those struggles that
demand more firmness and courage than to face the cannon.   The warning is all the more terrible when we see

that so omnipotent is the tyranny of this habit of intoxication that even his firmness and courage, remarkable as they were, failed at last. He was widely known, and his life story will have a wide and valuable influence."

The Hon. Henry Wilson, United States Senator, has written the following : —

"I am gratified to learn that a life of our dear but unfortunate friend Uniac has been prepared.

" You knew him well, knew how he was tempted and tried, and the sad story of his fall and death.

"You will, I am sure, trace the life of this gifted brother with fidelity to truth.

"It will be a story of tender interest to his personal friends, and to the thousands who have so often tearfully listened to his eloquent appeals for total abstinence, and warnings against the tempter, under whose insidious influence he fell and perished.

" Very respectfully,
"HENRY WILSON."

Rev. Gilbert Haven, D. D., editor "Zion's Herald," has given us the following : —

"I hear with pleasure that Mr. —— is preparing a life of Mr. E. H. Uniac. Mr. Uniac was a brilliant man, whose subjugation to the fearful appetite for strong drink caused a sad termination of his career. His life is full of lessons suited to the hour, and we believe its publication will be of great benefit to all who are under the dominion of strong drink, as well as to the young and rising generation.

                                              "G. Haven."

The Rev. D. C. Eddy, D. D.   "I am glad you intend writing the story of poor Uniac. Gifted but unfortunate, his life is a lesson to our young men. God grant they may heed it."

J. H. Orne, Esq., Past Right Worthy Grand Templar of North America, of the order of Good Templars, has given his estimate of Uniac, as follows : —

                    "Marblehead, Mass., Oct. 6, 1870.

"Dear Sir, — I am glad to hear that you have engaged to write the 'life' of the lamented Uniac. The striking incidents of his early life, his career as a soldier in the Union armies, his noble struggles for emancipation from the bondage of intemperance, his rapid rise from obscurity to distinction as an orator and public speaker, his devoted services for the benefit of his fellow-man, and the sad closing of his brilliant career, have excited the interest of hundreds who were proud to acknowledge him as a friend. You knew him better than any of us, for he was your *companion*, as well as friend, in labors for the advancement of the cause, which he gratefully acknowledged had led him to a higher and better life ; and if you record the strange incidents of his eventful life with entire fidelity, you cannot fail to produce a work that shall be an eloquent lesson of encouragement to others.

                    "Yours truly,

                              "J. H. Orne."

CHAPTER XIX.

REVIEW — LESSONS OF HIS LIFE — STRENGTH OF APPE-
TITE — ESTIMATES OF LIQUOR TRAFFIC — PROGRESS OF
REFORM, ETC.

WE have been tracing a life full of warning and in-
struction.   We have tried to so present it as to do
entire justice to the dead, and at the same time benefit
the living.

Who can read this history of a single life, and see the
grand opportunities lost, the hopes of friends disappointed, and everything bright turned into darkness,
without feeling impressed with the startling truth that
this is a representative case of many others scattered·all
over the land, who are to-day going through the same
struggles and trials that he went through, and will go
down as he went down?   And what thinking man can
look at these facts, connected with this one life alone, and
not be impressed with the truth that this question of
temperance is the most profound and important one now
before the American people?   If, in the gathering together of incidents and facts in this work, we have seemed
to repeat and linger over this or that idea, in connection
with this struggling life, we have done it to endeavor,
if possible, to impress more and more on the minds and
hearts of our American youth, the terrible situation

this man who was more than usually brilliant, occupied,
because of his own free and voluntary act in the early
years of his life, — he putting to his lips that which
fatally injured and enslaved him.

There are several lessons to be learned from this history ; and the first one we see that affected this man's
whole after career, was the want of proper associates and
influences in the moulding period of his life. In his youthful days, had he remained under the roof of his native
home till he had become fixed in his habits, perhaps his
whole life would have been changed for the better; at
any rate, mothers and fathers, you cannot be too careful
for the welfare of your boys in this direction. One day
we visited, in company with Uniac, the Massachusetts
State Prison, and in one of the shops, the officer said,
" Do you see that man sitting yonder?" We looked and
saw a man in the prime of life, with a sad-looking coun-
tenance, and the officer said that man belonged to one of
our best families, and left his home when fourteen years
of age ; and, coming to Boston, he fell into bad company,
and, going from step to step, he at last committed a crime
which will keep him here for fifteen years ; and the officer said he had heard him say, time after time, as tears
ran down his cheeks, " all, all came from my yielding to
the requirements of bad associates whom I would have
scorned to admit into my society when at home." There
is nothing remarkable about this incident ; it is a common
one, alas, too common ! but it shows the great importance
of the point of which we have spoken.

The next truth that forces itself home to our judgment and candor is, that it is the imperative duty of every

man who to-day has the power to stop the use of intoxicating liquors, who sees the habit growing on him, to do
it at once. We do not attempt to say there may not be
cases when a man has taken the first glass, and thereby
aroused a sleeping or innate desire which perhaps was
inherited by him from some dissipated ancestor, — for
there are those who have given this subject much thought
and investigation, who contend that this appetite or love
for drink is transmitted from one generation to the
other; and in this sense are the "sins of the fathers
visited upon the children, even to the third and fourth
generation."

If, then, there are so many chances that your children,
if they come in contact with alcoholic drinks, may be
injured and lost, can we do less than remove from their
sight and reach everything of this nature? Had Uniac
lived where the public sentiment would not tolerate the
traffic in liquor, of course it is safe to assert again what
we have intimated in other parts of this book, that he
would have lived a sober man, and died an upright and
honored citizen. Some contend that we show the reformed men too much sympathy. They would sound in
his ears, night and day, "No drunkard shall enter the
kingdom of Heaven." They would enforce the truth on
his mind that it is a sin to give way to his appetite. We
do not doubt but that there may be cases of mis-
placed sympathy, and where men are not deserving of it;
but it is impossible for us to feel that all men who yield
to appetite should come under this condemnation. When
we are looking at the actions of a man's life, we usually
try and see what his motives were for this or that action.

And who can find a single *good* reason or motive for the fall of Uniac, in any other way except that his appetite overcame his will, almost if not entirely against his desire.

Judge Crosby, of Lowell, has sometime during the last twelve months made a speech before a committee of the Massachusetts Legislature, in which he contends there is throughout the land a false sympathy which is injuring the virtues and morals of the people, — that we do not give men who sin to understand and feel that they have sinned and done wrong, and that they must be punished for violating the laws of God and man. We have not here attempted to present anything more than an idea of the drift of his argument. We have also noticed that one or two papers, in alluding to this matter, have taken the same view of the subject. But if there were only this case of Uniac to sustain the view we have taken, we should feel justified in standing by the truth of what we have presented, in regard to the power of appetite over him, and those like him; but there are hundreds and thousands of cases all over the country to confirm this position. The Rev. W. H. H. Murray, in a lecture delivered at Music Hall recently, said that he had seen men so much under the control and power of appetite that even the *smell* of brandy in pies or puddings might awake their slumbering appetite, and send them back to their old habits.

It might be interesting to continue this discussion further; for it seems certain that when the people awake to the terrible reality that there is the remotest danger of any one that they love ever coming under the dominion of this power, they will arise in their might and put it out of their way, and crush it beneath their feet.

Uniac has done his work. His mission under God doubtless will serve to show the truth of this danger, and the young men of this age and country be made to feel how awful is the evil of intemperance; and we trust it will have the effect to lead them to resolve, as for them and theirs, they will not touch or taste anything of this character while life lasts. We are living in a grand and glorious age, — in a time when great opportunities are opening up on every hand, — and we cannot afford to wait for the chiselled marble to record the fact that we lived and died, with date of the same. Grander far is the sublime ambition to write your own epitaph on the beating heart of humanity by uniform uprightness of character, abstinence from foolish indulgence, and an earnest desire to benefit mankind. Let the young man who sighs for something to do which shall make his name known and honored through life, look about him; for the cry on every breeze is for *men*, — men with souls and bodies baptized with a love for God and poor weak humanity, — men and true women who will go forth into the harvest field of the world's great garden and labor. How many men like Uniac need your kind words and gentle acts. Yes, the young and rising need to be taught, as you teach their infant lips to pray, that this demon is lurking in their pathway, and they must shun and avoid it. Men will tell you perhaps that this temperance reform is only the wild dream of some crazy fanatic, that it will perish and fade away in a little while. Do not be deceived; for in the beautiful words of another

we say, "The reform will go on. From whatever standpoint you may look at it, it will be seen to be in exact
harmony with the age. It *must* go on. God has written
it. Its champions are not fanatics. They are terribly
in earnest. Back of them are memories that will not
let them pause in the great work they have taken hold
of."

I remember one evening, as Uniac was closing a speech
during an exciting campaign, some one in his audience
cried out, "O, that is all stuff." Uniac caught the words
and straightening himself up to his full height, said,
"Young man, do you tell me that, when I have seen the
misery of family after family, — when I have looked on
genius in rags, innocence clothed in filth, — when I
have seen the noblest and best of earth carried down by
the dark waters of intemperance, that this is only stuff?
God forbid that you should ever see what I have gazed
upon, or feel the iron enter, hot and burning into your
very soul; but, my young friend, if you ever are thus
abused, you will not call this reform ' stuff.' " Thus we
find occasionally people who have not spent one hour in
the whole course of their lives to honestly investigate this
question, who seem to think we are radical and unreasonable when we demand the attention and decisive action
of men. There is a class who believe that in the economy
of God certain men are doomed to be drunkards, and we
must regulate the traffic, and throw around it the appearance of respectability, and when a man like Uniac lets his
appetite run away with his judgment, as they say, why
provide some home or place for him, — while to a man
who has spent any time in the investigation of this mat-

ter, the cold indifference of some such good and true men is, in other respects, more than they can understand or give a reason for.

When the men who look on the temperance reform as of no consequence, — when they shall begin to *feel* it in some way, — begin to understand something of the immense power there is in the rum-shops of America, then perhaps they will see the need of the temperance work and education we are laboring for to-day.

Uniac's life and death is perhaps one of the best illustrations of the power of appetite that we have had for years brought out to the full view of the people, and at the same time plainly shows us how the rum power is ruining the noblest and the best.

If by this life of a man many loved to honor, we can gather information, surely by his death, he who went down fighting, we ought to get something which shall awaken every heart, soul, and mind to the duty of the hour.

And though there are times when the work will seem hard, when we will feel like giving up in despair, and sitting down by the road-side, we shall soon see a rift in the darkest clouds, for God's hand is under and above all.

It may not be without some benefit, if in the closing of a story where the power of the appetite for liquor carried a man down to his death, to glance at the extent and strength of the liquor traffic in the United States.

By referring to a report of an officer connected with the revenue department of our government, we find the following startling figures. The sale of liquor in this

14

country for the year ending June 30th, 1871, was as follows: —

Of whiskey there was sold sixty million gallons, and at six dollars a gallon, it would amount to three hundred and sixty millions of dollars. Imported spirits were two million five hundred thousand gallons, which, sold at ten dollars per gallon, would make the amount of twenty-five million dollars. Imported wine, ten million seven hundred thousand gallons, which if sold at five dollars per gallon would bring fifty-three million five hundred thousand dollars, and ale, beer, and porter we find to have been about one hundred and thirty million dollars worth. Native wines are estimated at thirty-one million five hundred thousand dollars worth, making a grand total of over six hundred millions of dollars. What an amount of money, most of it worse than wasted.

There are supposed to be about one hundred and sixty thousand liquor dealers in this country. How much good they might accomplish if their labors were turned into some useful channel.

The following will give us still further figures: —

From the report of Commissioner Delano, we find that the whole number of distilleries registered last year was 770, with a spirit-producing capacity of 910,551 gallons every twenty-four hours, making for ten months — the period usually run — 203,912,800 gallons. The revenue collections from spirits alone amounted to $55,581,599.18; fermented liquors, $6,319,126.90; receipts from tobacco,

$31,350,707.88; total revenue, $185,235,817.97; thus making from whiskey and tobacco nearly one-half of the entire revenue. The whole amount of spirits in market Nov. 15, 1870, was 45,637,993 gallons, of which 36,619-968 gallons were out of bond, and 9,018,924 gallons in Government warehouses.

The following are the approximate receipts for the year ending June 30, 1871.

APPROXIMATE RECEIPTS FOR THE FISCAL YEAR 1871.

Spirits.

Brandy distilled from apples, grapes, and peaches....	$1,416,008 21
Spirits distilled from materials other than apples, grapes, and peaches..............................	29,743,974 82
Distilleries, per diem tax on	1,901,202 54
Distillers' special tax................................	5,681,346 75
Rectifiers...	959,703 08
Dealers, retail liquor..	3.651,576 51
" wholesale liquor	2,149,916 03
Manufacturers of stills, and stills and worms manufactured.......................................	5,823 16
Stamps, distillery warehouse, for rectified spirits, etc.	759,360 01
Excess of gaugers' fees	13.544 21
Total spirits	$46,282,463 82

Fermented Liquors.

Fermented liquors, tax of $1 per barrel on	$7,159,333 85
Brewers' special tax..............................	229,807 87
Total fermented liquors	$7,389,141 72
Total...................................	$53,671,615 54

From the above facts, we get an idea of the immense

power of a traffic that can afford to pay such heavy amounts of revenue tax, and then roll up colossal fortunes upon the profits of the business.

The tax and profit, together with the original cost of manufacture, must come out of the pockets of the drinkers, who spend the larger portion of their wages in this unprofitable way; and in view of these truths can we wonder that there are hard cases of poverty in almost every part of our land, that come from the squandering of money in the direction of buying liquor?

When on the 17th of March Uniac fell, he had quite a sum of money put away, and in the short space of four weeks he had spent every dollar, and pledged his watch for rum; and it is from men like this that many men to-day are laying up large fortunes. We need to place these facts before the people whenever we can, for while men are debating how to pay off the war debt, they fail to see how their taxes are affected by the sale of liquor; but some one will answer that the government derives a large revenue amount from the tax on liquor; granted — but does any one who gives the subject a moment's thought, think we do not pay out double the amount to support and take care of the men and women whose lives come under its power? We have visited ten or twelve State prisons in various parts of our land, and in every instance, the officers have said to us, " At least nine-tenths of all the prisoners under my charge are here, either directly or indirectly, because of the use of intoxicating liquors." We also see by the reports of men who have in charge the poor of our States, that four out of five are reduced to poverty because of rum, and facts could be shown proving that at least three-fourths of all the business of our criminal courts, and of the services of our judges and officers of courts, as well as the policemen, are necessary, because of rum-selling and rum-drinking. I ask, then, the men who believe in allowing the sale of liquor because of the revenue it brings to the government, to foot up the cost of taking care of nine out of ten of your prisoners, of supporting four out of five of your paupers, of paying the salary of your court officers, to say nothing of various other ways that might be mentioned, where men pay money to take care of the victims of rum selling and drinking, and then render in how much net is made to the tax-payers of our country, by the revenue on liquors. Beside this tremendous array of figures and facts in a financial line, look for a moment at another estimate in another direction. By careful men who have given the best of attention to the matter, we find that one hundred thousand lives are annually lost by intemperance, two hundred thousand children sent to the poor-house, one hundred thousand men and women sent to prisons, two hundred thousand children made worse than orphans, and an army of six hundred thousand drunkards tremble and totter through the streets of our nation ; three hundred and fifty thousand persons are employed in connection with the liquor traffic. We have more than four dram-shops to *one* school, two million of children in the United States do not attend school, a large majority of whom are detained by the influence of rum. This is but a casual summary of the great traffic that is carrying down in its mighty grasp men like him whom we have been following from

step to step, till the black waters closed over him. But
is there no bright side to all this dark shading?   I
thank God, we can answer, yes! The great wave of
progress is rolling ever and on, and though it may be
impeded for a season, it will have no permanent delay,
for the pulpit, platform, and press have touched the public heart throughout the length and breadth of the land.
Public opinion is steadily advancing in the right direction.   Here and there a laborer may prove false to his
obligation, but others from the young will come forward
to take his place, and the movement of the hour is
forward.   There was an age in the history of the world,
when "God wills it!" was the watchword that summoned kings, barons, and princes from their castles
and thrones; when peasants from their dens and hov-
els all hastened to join the crusade.   It was the
one grand heart-heaving of the age, and every pulse
beat responsive to the word.   Every age since
has had its watchword and inspiration; and has this
age nothing to inspire and push us forward? Yes, on
every breeze, in every department of active life, comes
the magic word "Progress"; faster and faster is the cry
of the hour, and God will help us carry on this glorious
reform so that it shall keep pace with the watchword of
the age, if we are faithful.   But there is work to do and
prayers to be offered before we shall see that substantial
progress which we so much hope for and desire.   What
is our army composed of?   Who are to open up the way?
In North America we have, in addition to all the open
organizations and churches, Sunday-schools, Bands of
Hope, and other societies dedicated to this work, three

hundred **and** fifty-seven thousand one hundred and nineteen Good Templars who are pledged to total abstinence and prohibition, one hundred and seventeen thousand five hundred and four Sons of Temperance, and seventeen thousand five hundred and more members of the Temple of Honor, also pledged to the same principles. Here are a half a million men and women in these three organizations alone, who, if true to temperance on every occasion, will ere long purify our land and "make our streets pure and safe" for men like Uniac to walk in, as well as to prevent the young from ever coming near the contaminating influence of the flaming fluid.

While with tearful eyes and sad hearts we contemplate how many must in the deep despair of their souls, like Uniac, cry to have the burden lifted from their bleeding hearts ; while —

> " Man's inhumanity to man
> Makes countless thousands mourn,"

we shall see hours, when it will be indeed hard to press on, we shall see men over whom we have watched and labored, drawn into temptation and again be stripped of their manhood, we shall stand by bedsides of other noble and gifted men, and hear them with their dying breath curse this traffic ; we shall see men who are dealing in this human poison petted and honored, and we shall see friends who by our exertions have been lifted to places of honor and trust betraying the cause, — we shall see and feel all this, and perhaps more. But we shall also see homes made happy by the onward wave of this reform.

We shall see husbands restored to their wives, and chil
dren made happy; we shall feel the consciousness of
duty done; we shall know that though the wicked may
for a time seem to flourish and spread themselves like a
mighty tree, that in a little while they will be cut down
and perish. We shall see men who for the love of the
cause will be willing to sacrifice and endure anything in
the line of duty; we shall ere long catch the music that
will be wafted to our waiting ears from the golden chime-
bells of that age foretold by prophets of old, and seen in
vision by men who were suffering in gloomy dungeons
for the sake of principle. Yes, we shall see in this free
America, best of all the " coming man" with godlike form
and unshaken step doing his duty, not for office nor place
nor for self, but for the good of his fellow-man and for the
honor of God; we shall see this "coming man" not
under the influence of wine, and clinging to false and dangerous ideas of social customs and fashionable follies.
But our representative American of the future shall be as
a man who, having become purified from the taint of that
which we so much lament, and being ready to use his
right as a citizen at the ballot-box in the direction of
sustaining a government founded on the principle of true
liberty, where no man shall have the right to traffic in
the bodies and souls of his fellows; the man who shall
vote as he prays, — who shall lift up and find no dram-
shop to drag down. If this portrait of the American
of the future is not overdrawn, if the time is coming
when all men who expect to hold places of trust and
honor shall feel that they must in their lives and pro-
fessions be true to this matter, then is there indeed hope
for the future.

The struggle between rum and temperance, between license and prohibition, must go on, till, from the golden shores of the Pacific to the storm-beat Atlantic coast there shall be no spot of earth above which waves the American flag where men shall perish as Uniac did.

O, by this man's struggles, by his bitter tears, by his thrilling words of personal experience, by his eventful life and untimely death, — we indict the liquor traffic of the land, we charge upon it his blood, and the blood and agony of thousands of other burdened hearts, — by all this we hope and pray that our people will not only sustain the indictment, but convict and sentence this wrong to banishment forever from the earth.

www.ingramcontent.com/pod-product-compliance
Lightning Source LLC
Chambersburg PA
CBHW030128030726
47498CB00007B/2597